D0277109

**This book is to be returned on or before
the last date stamped below.**

North Ayrshire Libraries

MOST ITEMS CAN BE RENEWED BY TELEPHONE

THE OLIVE GROVE

THE
OLIVE GROVE

Evelyn Hood

This title first published in Great Britain 1998 by
SEVERN HOUSE PUBLISHERS LTD of
9–15 High Street, Sutton, Surrey SM1 1DF.
Originally published in 1982 by Mills & Boon under the title
A Time To Care and pseudonym of *Elizabeth A. Webster.*
First published in the USA 1998 by
SEVERN HOUSE PUBLISHERS INC., of
595 Madison Avenue, New York, NY 10022.

British Library Cataloguing in Publication Data

Hood, Evelyn, 1936-
      The olive grove
      1. Love stories
      1.   Title II. Webster, Elizabeth A., 1936-. Time to care
823.9'14 [F]

      ISBN 0-7278-2204-7

Printed and bound in Great Britain by
MPG Books Ltd, Bodmin, Cornwall.

Author's Note

The storyline of *The Olive Grove* began to develop during a perfect holiday in Corfu, a very beautiful and romantic island.

One of the pleasures of being a novelist lies in being able to revisit places in the mind, while writing about them. When the holiday was over I very much wanted to transport myself back to Corfu's blue skies, its white-walled houses dreaming beneath the sun, the quiet little bays where the water was so clear that the boats looked as though they were suspended in glass, and the water itself, warm and soft as silk and a delight to swim in. I also wanted to write about the people – handsome, spirited and possessed of a strong sense of identity and history.

As to the book itself, I believe strongly that the keenest, most difficult conflict is not between two people, but within one person forced to choose between what she wants and what she believes. Sara finds her employer's half-brother Patrick the most exciting and attractive man she has ever met, but Patrick flits from woman to woman, while Sara believes absolutely in love, marriage and fidelity. As her feelings for Patrick strengthen, her inner conflict threatens to tear her apart.

As for love – it is one of the strongest, most powerful emotions known to the human race. Put love and conflict together, and a story is born. Writing *The Olive Grove* took me back to Corfu, and I became very involved in Sara's story. And as far as Patrick is concerned – I fell as deeply in love with him as Sara was, and enjoyed every minute of it!

Evelyn Hood, 1998

CHAPTER ONE

A SHARP rattle of small stones cascading down a rocky slope broke the silence.

Sara opened her eyes, dazed. Through dark glasses she could make out a huge figure silhouetted between her and the strong sun. With a gasp she sat up on the flat rock and whipped the glasses off.

'Good morning——' a deep, pleasant voice greeted her in Greek. She blinked, dazzled by the light, unable to see who had interrupted her peace.

'What—what do you want?'

'I'm sorry,' he said in English. 'Did I startle you?'

Her eyes became accustomed to the glare, as he jumped down from a rock on to the shingle beach and stood before her, hands on hips. Broad-shouldered and tall, dark hair in an untidy mop about a brown face, white teeth gleaming in a grin, he looked, in faded blue tee-shirt and shabby jeans, like a modern pirate. At any other time Sara might have found him attractive. Now, she was confused and embarrassed as they surveyed each other. Colour rose in her cheeks as his blue eyes moved slowly over her body. Clearly, he enjoyed

looking—and admired what he saw. Thank goodness, she found herself thinking, she had put on
the top half of her yellow bikini after swimming
semi-nude.

'I suppose you know you're trespassing?'

He raised one dark eyebrow. 'Am I, now?'

Sara reached for her white towelling robe, and
to her annoyance found that it was out of reach,
almost at the stranger's feet. He bent and picked
it up. 'Is this what you want?'

'Give it to me, please.'

He hesitated, holding the robe between his
fingers, while his eyes travelled once again over
her slim brown body. Then, at last, he murmured
regretfully, 'Well—if you insist!'

With the robe on, she felt braver.

'How did you get on to this beach?' she asked.

He nodded at the path on the other side of the
shingle.

'From the road? Perhaps you didn't know that
it's private.' As he said nothing, but continued to
stand where he was, smiling at her, she hurried
on. 'It belongs to that villa up on the hill.'

He glanced up to where the villa's white walls
could be glimpsed through the trees. 'And you're
the lady of the villa, are you?'

'No, I'm——' she checked herself. Why tell this
man anything? 'I'm a guest,' she said instead, a
haughty note creeping into her voice. 'What were
you doing here?'

The smile deepened. 'Just—admiring the view,'

he said innocently, indicating the shingle, the sea, the rocks—and swinging his attention back almost at once to Sara. Following his gaze, she looked down and saw that the neck of the robe had opened, exposing the soft curve of her breasts. She pulled the towelling shut, raging inwardly at her lack of height and the necessity to tilt her chin to look up at him.

'You didn't know that it was private?'

'What? Oh—the beach, you mean? No, I didn't. It doesn't look private, does it?' he asked conversationally, putting one sneakered foot on the edge of the rock she had been sunbathing on. 'I think it's too bad that the world has to be divided up among people. We should all be able to enjoy places like this beach, shouldn't we? After all—'

The conversation was getting out of hand. 'Mrs Laird owns the villa, and this land, she doesn't like tourists!' She could hear her own voice sharp and nagging, but was unable to control it. He stiffened, and his eyes became a clear blue flame. 'Now look here, Miss High and Mighty——'

Sara retreated a step, and stumbled as her foot hit a rock. She was saved from falling by two strong, sure hands on her shoulders.

'See what a burst of temper can do?' the stranger asked sympathetically. The smile returned as he looked down on her. 'You shouldn't let yourself get so—so excited,' he reproved, as though she was a naughty child.

She stood stiffly in his grasp. 'Will you please let me go?'

'Well——' his fingers moved as though to shape themselves more comfortably to the curve of her shoulders, and for a brief moment she was drawn closer to him. The robe fell open again, and there was admiration in his glance. Fear caught at Sara's mind. The beach was secluded, and she was the only person who used it. If she had to scream for help, would they hear her at the villa——?

As though sensing her thoughts the stranger released her and stepped back. 'If that's what you really want,' he said lightly, his smile mocking.

'Yes, it is. And I'd really like you to go. The path is over there.'

He didn't bother to look. 'I know. I came down it half an hour ago.'

'You—oh!' She almost dropped the towel and beach bag that she had just picked up. So he had been there all the time—had watched her swim, watched her walk out of the water with only the bottom half of the bikini on. Her breasts, now securely hidden beneath the robe, tingled with the thought of his gaze.

As though reading her mind, he said quietly, intimately, 'You were well worth seeing,' then turned and walked unhurriedly across the shingle, disappearing up the path to the road without a backward glance.

When Sara was sure that he had gone she sat down on the warm rock again to collect her thoughts before going back to the villa. The water sparkled invitingly, the beach was as enchanting as ever, the sun as hot as it had been before; but for the moment Corfu had lost its attraction, lost it before the mocking gaze of blue eyes that had studied her and indicated that what they saw was acceptable.

'Like a sultan in a slave-market!' Sara thought angrily, collecting her belongings once more. She took her time climbing the path that led from the beach, through trees and bushes that sheltered her from the sun's heat, to the garden. Small pale flowers clustered round the tree trunks, happy in the shade, and as she went up the steps to the garden, a lizard winked a jewelled eye at her from the stone wall, then disappeared with a flick of its tail.

Spiros, the man who came each day to look after the garden, was watering it when she reached the top of the steps. The foliage sparkled in the sunlight, dripping gems on to the flagstones below, and the air smelled fresh and moist. The villa was white-walled with blue shutters at the windows, and it was sheltered from the roadway by trees, giving it complete seclusion.

As she walked from the hot sunlight into the cool, tiled hall, Sara marvelled again at the good fortune that had whisked her away from England in September to this island in the sun. Her good fortune—but not Nicky's, for it was his accident that had given her the chance to come and work for him in Corfu.

He called to her as she crossed the hall, and she turned and went into the large downstairs room that he used as a study and bedroom.

Nicky was at his desk, with Sophia by his side. Her long slender fingers, each beautifully shaped and tipped with coral polish, were flipping through a notebook.

Nicky looked up, his face clearing, as Sara went in.

'Sara! Listen, love, do you know where the notes about the Coronation got to? Sophie can't find them anywhere, and neither can I.'

'In the filing cabinet.' Sara crossed to the metal cabinet by the wall. Nicky was out of his wheelchair and walking with a stick, but he still needed help when it came to finding papers. He always had—even when he was perfectly fit and she had done agency work for him in London.

'But here it says Coro—Coronation,' Sophia insisted, stumbling over the unusual word. Her English was almost perfect.

'Those notes are new, still to be typed and filed,' Sara explained. 'Here's the folder you want, Nicky.'

'Bless you!' he said happily, and a frown passed over Sophia's lovely face.

'I had to try to help Nikos, because you were nowhere to be found,' she said spitefully.

'I was on the beach.'

'She's entitled to have some time off, Sophia,'

Nicky told his cousin absentmindedly, his eyes on the folder Sara had handed him. 'Just my luck to get landed with a film script dealing with the Plantagenets,' he complained mildly. 'Now, if it had been the re-write of a modern book, I'd have had no problem.'

'I thought that Sara had come to Corfu as your secretary,' Sophia persisted sulkily.

Nicky tossed a lock of fair hair out of his eyes, frowning. 'Sophie, Sara's not an employee, and you know it. Stop being so silly!'

The Greek girl's mouth tightened, and she flounced from the room, leaving a trace of expensive perfume behind her. Looking after her, Sara wished once again that she had Sophia's tall elegance and grace. She could even flounce beautifully.

'I'll get some more of this typed for you as soon as I've changed.' She picked up one of the sheets of paper from his desk. It was covered with tiny, neat writing, for Nicky hated to type.

'Hmmm?' He looked up from the paper he was reading. His eyes widened, and he whistled approvingly. 'Hey—not bad! Why don't you just stay like that? You'd brighten the place up.'

There was admiration in his gaze, but it was—civilised admiration, Sara told herself, remembering the man on the beach.

'I don't think your mother would like that, Nicky.'

'I don't suppose she would—but who cares?

You know, Sara, you're one of the very few women who can look good with no make-up and wet hair?'

'Flattery,' said Sara firmly, 'will get you nowhere. Nor will it get your book typed,' and she escaped to her room to have a shower and get dressed. But she was lighthearted as she dropped the yellow bikini on the floor and looked at herself in the full-length mirror. As a film writer, Nicky was used to seeing beautiful women all the time. A compliment from him meant something.

If only, Sara thought, I could be a bit taller! She realised that she had a nice figure—not too curvy, but not too flat either. And with the tan that she had got since arriving in Corfu, she looked good. But not as good as Sophia.

'Which is why she's a model, and you're only an agency typist,' Sara remarked to her reflection, and went into the shower.

She changed into a sleeveless gold-coloured dress with a pleated skirt and plain V-neck, slipped on white sandals, and brushed her hair out. It was almost dry. A touch of rose-coloured lipstick and a dash of light perfume, and she was ready. The gold dress picked up the tawny glow in her wide brown eyes, and her hair shone.

'You can't have everything,' her mother told her repeatedly when she was a little girl. Well, she might not be beautiful, but she wasn't ugly. And she was the envy of all the girls in the typing agency where she worked.

Nicky Laird used the agency when he needed secretarial work done. After a while, he began to ask for Sara by name, and she enjoyed typing film scripts for him, helping with research, coping with his correspondence.

Because he divided his time between London and Greece, where his mother's home was, Nicky had no wish to employ a full-time secretary. The agency suited him very well, and he appreciated Sara. When he was convalescing at his mother's Corfu home after a car crash, with a deadline to meet, he had immediately contacted the agency and asked for Sara to be flown out to help him.

For her, it was a working holiday with a dreamlike quality to it. Three weeks after landing at the flower-decked airport, she still had to pinch herself now and then to make sure that she wasn't imagining it all.

'I hope you won't be lonely here,' Hermione Laird had said stiffly on Sara's first day at the villa. 'I have a great deal of business to see to. I have to spend a lot of time away from home. And Nikos, of course, needs rest. He should not be working.'

It was clear that this Greek woman, still handsome though her hair was liberally streaked with grey and her figure was running to fat, did not approve of her son's determination to go on working.

'I enjoy being alone—and I'll take care to see

that Mr Laird isn't overtired,' Sara had assured
her quietly.

'Hmmm.' The flashing dark eyes looked Sara
over. 'I find it surprising, Miss Weston, that a
woman so young and—attractive as you are
should be willing to come here on her own, away
from all her friends.'

There was curiosity in the woman's voice, but
Sara only made some light remark, and the
moment passed. She wasn't going to tell this dis-
approving woman, or anyone else at the villa, how
well timed Nicky's summons had been.

The mere thought of Richard was humiliating.
The pain was easing now, but the bitterness was
still there. She knew that she would never forget
the anger in his face, the scorn in his voice, during
their last meeting.

Like a fool, she had expected a proposal of marriage. Instead, he had suggested a weekend away
together, before he left for his new job in Australia.
Wide-eyed, innocent Sara, looking for white veiling
and orange-blossom. Sophisticated Richard, seeth-
ing when she turned him down angrily.

'Little Miss Mouse!' he had said scathingly.
'Where did you spring from, Sara? The Middle
Ages? I can certainly get what I want without mar-
riage—and if you're not available, that's that!'

She had thought then of leaving the flat she
shared with two other girls, thought of going
home to her family where she could nurse her
hurt pride in solitude. But Nicky had intervened,

and she was grateful to him for the opportunity
to rebuild her life away from the curious questions
of her flatmates.

Recalling her gratitude, she smiled warmly at
him as she went back into his room.

'Nice,' he approved, looking up and seeing her
in the doorway. 'You suit that colour. Look, Sara,
could you make a start on that lot? I've got to re-
write this scene—if I send that to Amy she'll go
mad. The lines are ridiculous!'

'Don't overdo things,' she cautioned, and he
frowned. 'You've been listening to Hermione
again, haven't you?'

'She cares about you, Nicky——'

'And nags you to death about it. Look, love,
you know as well as I do that this script has to be
in Amy's hands in six weeks' time—all checked,
finished, neatly typed and tied with a red ribbon.
I still think it would have been more sensible to
have flown back home to London. At least I'd
have got peace to get on with it there. Hermione
insisted on me staying here, and she can take the
consequences. I'm not an invalid, though she likes
to pretend that I am.'

'Perhaps you're not as bad as she thinks. But I
don't think you're as fit as you think, either.'

He shook his head. 'Sara, you're here to type,
not to nursemaid me. So—type!'

Obediently she sat down at the small desk which
held her typewriter. Nicky had always been pale-
skinned and fair-haired, but there was still a

drawn look about him that told of the pain he had suffered after his accident. He had explained to Sara that he resembled his English father rather than his dark Greek mother. It was very clear to see that he was the apple of his mother's eyes, that she wanted him to settle down in Greece with her. It was equally clear that he preferred life in England, and, Sara suspected, felt frustrated and suffocated by his mother's demands. She wondered from time to time why he didn't break loose. But Nicky was a gentle man, and he would be reluctant to upset his mother.

Hermione Laird arrived back home an hour later, sweeping unannounced into the room. She always wore a lot of gold jewellery, and the clatter of bracelets accompanied her into the room.

'Nikos, still working? You look pale——' She swooped down on him, cupping his face with her stubby, beringed hands.

'I'm all right, Hermione!' he said impatiently. But after dinner he admitted to feeling tired, and went to bed early. Sophia came downstairs, radiant in a peacock-blue dress with a fringed gold wrap. She was being taken to a night-club in Corfu Town by one of her many admirers.

'Out again?' Hermione frowned. Sara had an idea that behind her hostess's plan to invite Sophia to the villa for a rest after an arduous season modelling clothes, there was a scheme to throw Nicky and the Greek girl together. With a Greek wife, he might settle down in his mother's country. But Nicky and Sophia had shown little interest in each other.

'Perhaps I should ask the doctor to call tomorrow and see Nikos,' Hermione fretted when she and Sara were alone.

'But he's only tired.'

'I suppose so.' Hermione paced the lounge, fidgeting with her necklace. 'Oh, that terrible accident! When I see what it has done to my Nikos!' At any moment, Sara thought, suppressing a giggle, her hostess would break into an operatic aria. 'If only Patrick hadn't persuaded him to go in the car that day. I didn't even know, at first. I thought that Patrick was alone, when first I heard of the accident——'

'Patrick?'

The older woman's mouth tightened. 'My—stepson, Nikos's half-brother. It was he who decided that they should all go in his new car—Patrick and Nikos and their friend Stavros. Patrick always had to show off his new toys—women, cars, it made no difference. He always had to be better than everyone else. And Nikos always believed him! And then——' the drama was gone and real horror showed in her eyes as she relived the moment, '—then the car went off the road. Stavros was killed, leaving a young widow. My Nikos was so badly injured that at first we thought he might never walk again.'

'And Patrick?'

Hermione shrugged. 'Patrick? He escaped with

a few bruises and sprains. It was my Nikos who
had to suffer the pain, the months of agony!'

It was obvious to Sara that Hermione would
have shed no tears if her renegade stepson had
been killed in the accident. Nor did she seem very
interested in the man who had died.

Nicky was still tired the following morning, and
his mother insisted that no work was done. Sara
finished the typing, brought the files up to date,
and decided to walk to the village.

Nicky was settled in a shady part of the garden,
a cool drink by his side, a book in his lap, cushions
behind his head.

'Sit down and talk to me, Sara. We haven't
really had a chance to get to know each other.'

His mother cut in quickly, 'If Sara wants to go
to the village, she can get some things for me.
Sophia will talk to you.'

Sophia, half asleep in a chair beside Nicky,
moved her slender shoulders in a shrug. She had
arrived back in the early hours of the morning,
and had breakfasted in her room. Even in a simple
white shirt and green slacks, brown eyes shaded
by sunglasses and her lovely honey-coloured hair
loose about her face, she was an exotic flower.

Sara turned down Hermione's offer of her car.
Her hostess rarely walked anywhere, and thought,
like Sophia, that it was peculiar of Sara to tramp
the mile to the village. But Sara needed her occasional walks, and her daily swim from the little
beach, to recharge her batteries. Even though life

at the villa was quiet, she didn't feel that she was alone there, able to relax.

The road was empty, apart from an occasional car or lorry. The bushes were white with dust and the still air was heavy with the scent of flowers. A priest passed her, solemn in his dark robes and grey beard, nodding his tall hat at her in greeting as he passed by. Women working in a field near the road kept up a continual conversation with each other, the rapid Greek that always sounded vibrantly alive flowing back and forth across the expanse between them. Although she couldn't understand the language, Sara felt very much at home on the island Corfu's unhurried pace, its breathtaking scenery and its beautiful, friendly people would remain in her memory for always.

The village consisted of one rough main street, with a few side lanes where the local people lived. Sara wandered round the small supermarket for a while, then stepped back on to the dazzling, dusty street. She went to the little taverna where she usually stopped for a drink. A door at the back opened on to a tiny patio, just large enough for three tables. The sandy beach was beyond the patio, and she sat and watched the happy, dark-eyed children playing round an upturned rowing boat as she sipped her drink. A few tourists tramped through the taverna, calling out a greeting to the patron, settling themselves at the other two tables, glancing curiously at Sara. Sometimes she made the most of the tourists she met and enjoyed their company—at other times, like today, she stayed silent, content to relax on her own.

At last she glanced at her watch. If she wanted to swim before the evening meal, she would have to start back to the villa. Stepping out of the taverna door, she shaded her eyes against the sun's glare, made to turn towards the villa—and stopped short. A short distance away the man from the beach, still in the same shabby tee-shirt and jeans, was about to climb into a battered-looking Land Rover.

Sara turned to flee, but he had already seen her.

'Hello there——' With a few strides of his long legs he had reached her, and was looming over her.

'I had a feeling that we might meet again. So you're not just a water nymph after all?'

'I beg your pardon?'

His eyes swept over her, setting up a tingle that reached down to her toes. She was wearing a navy-and-white striped cotton sweater with neat light blue jeans—but he had a way of looking at her as though she had nothing on at all, she realised with dismay and embarrassment.

'Yesterday, I wondered if you were real, or a Greek water nymph from the legends, when you walked out of the sea with your wet hair about your face and your skin gleaming——'

'I can assure you that I'm quite human,' she said quickly, icily. That maddening blush was warming her face again.

'Well, I felt that you must be when you started shouting at me. Nymphs don't shout. As far as I know, they——'

'I was not shouting!'

'Oh yes, you were. Pity—I've never actually met a goddess in the—the flesh.'

'If you don't mind——' she tried to push past him.

'Can I give you a lift?'

'No, I—I have shopping to do. Excuse me——' Panicking, she turned away and scurried into the supermarket. Her heart was pounding. If he followed her—or waited for her——

The cheerful little supermarket owner raised his eyebrows. 'You forgot?' he asked in his halting English. A basket of huge tomatoes stood on the counter, and Sara pointed at them. Anything would do.

The shopkeeper put the tomatoes into a bag and handed over change with a speed she had never seen before, it seemed. She ventured cautiously outside, and sighed with relief as she saw the Land Rover disappearing round a corner.

She kept her bikini top on as she waded into the crystal clear sea later that day. She loved swimming without it, loved the caressing touch of the water on her skin, the freedom. But, although the beach remained quite empty, her pleasure in her swim was spoiled. She came out of the water after a short time, fuming as she returned to the villa. It was maddening that one insolent man, one thoughtless fool, could ruin her serenity.

A wind blew up in the evening, one of those sudden gales that swept Corfu occasionally towards the end of summer. In the lounge, Hermione worked at her writing desk and Nicky and Sophia settled down to a game of backgammon. Sara stood for a while at the window, watching the trees bend against the might of the wind. She was always fascinated by the gales which were warm despite their ferocity, and which disappeared as quickly as they came, once they had finished amusing themselves with the trees and the sea.

A figure appeared at the double wrought iron gates, opened them, and came into the garden. Sara's eyes widened.

'Oh, no!' she murmured, one hand going to her throat. A man was nearing the house, his dark head bent against the wind, his hands thrust into the pockets of a bright red anorak. As he neared the door he looked up, eyes narrowed against the warm gust, and she saw that he had the face of a pirate.

Surely she wasn't going to be haunted by him for the rest of her stay in Corfu! She hurried from the room and went into the hall, praying that none of the others had noticed his coming. Really, this was going too far! She refused to let herself be pestered and embarrassed in front of Nicky and his mother!

She threw the door open just as his hand reached out for the elaborate silver bell that hung on the wall. He stared at her, blue eyes wide, dark, well-shaped brows lifted slightly.

'Either it's extra-sensory perception, or the sheer animal magnetism between us,' he said mildly. 'I hope you noted, by the way, that I arrived by the official, accepted route, not by trespassing on your private beach. I'm improving.'

'If you've come here to annoy me——'

He stepped on to the top step, towering over her, and she was aware, all at once, of the quiet strength of him. 'May I come in? It's a bit windy to annoy you out here.'

'Of course you can't come in!'

'You're honest, at any rate. No shilly-shallying, no maidenly fluttering—just a straight from-the-shoulder rejection. I like that. But I'd still like to come in—if you'll just stand aside?'

She tried to shut the door, but he put a large hand on it, and she was helpless.

'Will you please go away!' she hissed at him. 'My employer isn't likely to care for the idea of strangers calling on me and forcing their way in!'

The eyebrows rose again. 'Your employer? So you're not——'

'Who is it, Sara?' Hermione's imperious voice asked from the hallway behind Sara.

As she turned, the interloper took advantage of her momentary distraction. With one easy movement he opened the door wider, sweeping Sara back a few steps, and strode past her to stand in the hall, filling it with his height and his broad shoulders.

'It's just an uncouth trespasser,' he said cheerfully. 'Your guest here was doing her best to have me ejected, but I knew that you'd want to see me, Hermione.'

If Sara had been surprised and dismayed to see him, Hermione was both astounded and furious. A variety of expressions flitted across her face. She glanced quickly at the lounge behind her, as though hoping to keep its occupants in ignorance of the visitor. Then, after a few seconds, she forced a chill smile of welcome to her lips, though her eyes were stormy and her voice flat.

'Patrick! What are you doing on Corfu?'

CHAPTER TWO

IF Hermione Laird's greeting was less than warm, her stepson gave no sign that he had noticed. He strode forward and bent to kiss her cheek.

'Hello, Hermione,' he said breezily. 'It's been a long time.'

'Has it?' She allowed his lips to brush her cheek, then stepped back, eyes hostile. 'You'd—you'd better come in, Patrick.'

As Hermione turned towards the lounge, Patrick Laird raised an eyebrow at Sara. 'Well, coming? Or do they make you stand in the corner all the time?'

Aware that she had been watching in open-mouthed amazement, she shut the front door and swept past him into the room. Nicky glanced up, then a huge grin creased his face.

'Patrick! My golly, it's good to see you——' He struggled to get to his feet, reaching for the stick which rested against the arm of his chair. But Patrick was by his side at once, pushing him back down.

'Don't get up, it's only me. How are you, Nikos?'

As Nicky opened his mouth to reply, Hermione cut in. 'Making a very slow recovery!' From

where she stood by the door Sara saw the quick
movement of Patrick's head, and the throb of a
muscle in his jaw.

Colour rose in Nicky's pale face, and he darted
an angry look at his mother. 'Making a good recovery, Pat. I'm a fraud—I should have been back
in London weeks ago, but Hermione insisted on
babying me a bit longer.'

'I expect she enjoys it,' Patrick's deep voice said
easily. 'Sophie—I didn't know you were on
Corfu?'

Sophia leaned back in her chair, looked Patrick
up and down with easy familiarity. Sara wondered
if Patrick's gaze was scanning the Greek girl with
that appreciation which she remembered from
their meeting on the beach. And she knew, by the
sleepy curve of Sophia's lips and the way she
hooded her brown eyes, that her guess had been
right.

'Sophie's staying with us for a week or two,'
Nicky's voice was calm, but there was amusement
in the glance he divided between his half-brother
and Sophia.

All at once Sara knew that there had, at some
time, been something between Patrick and
Sophia, and that Nicky knew of it. They were
close, these three—they were sophisticated,
poised, while she was a non-starter. She felt
a flash of pain, and put it down to envy of
the three of them, rather than envy of Sophia
alone. A beautiful girl like Sophia would, of

course, attract a man like Patrick.

'And this is Sara Weston, who is also staying with us.'

Patrick swung round, and now it was Sara's turn to come under that vivid blue gaze once more. Her hand was imprisoned in a strong grip as Patrick said formally, 'How do you do?'

So he wasn't going to embarrass her after all! She lifted her chin, stared steadily up into his face, tried to slip her hand from his after an appropriate length of time—only to find it held fast.

'Haven't we met before?' he asked, and now she could see the laughter dancing in his gaze, and the twist of his lips.

'I don't think so.'

Dark brows knotted briefly. 'But I'm sure that—now I remember!' he said triumphantly. 'I met you on the beach the other day, didn't I?'

His fingers held hers gently, yet short of pulling away she could not release her hand. Colour rose in her face as she noticed Sophia's sudden interest in Patrick's words, and Nicky's surprise.

'I—I believe we did meet,' she said reluctantly, and at last he let her go. She moved quickly away, to sit on the sofa.

'On our beach?' Nicky was asking. 'You didn't mention it, Sara.'

Patrick smiled down on her. 'She didn't realise who I was, of course. I'm afraid I gave her a bit of a fright. You see, she was——'

'I was sunbathing,' Sara interrupted swiftly, too swiftly. 'We didn't exchange names.'

'I think she thought I was a gatecrashing fisherman, or possibly a tourist who had lost his way.'

'Coffee,' Nicky decided. 'You must have some coffee, Patrick. Sophia———?'

'Sara will attend to the coffee, I am sure,' Sophia's voice was light, impersonal. Her eyes brushed Sara, then returned to Patrick. Nicky frowned slightly and opened his mouth to speak, but Sara said at once, 'Of course———' and escaped to the kitchen.

Each day a woman from the village came in to attend to housework and cook the meals. In the evenings, she went home after preparing the evening meal, and they looked after themselves.

With fingers that trembled a little, Sara made coffee, set a tray with glazed brown coffee cups and saucers, ringed with gold. She hesitated, then defiantly added a fifth cup and saucer to the tray. She had planned to spend the rest of the evening in her room, but she realised now that it would only support Sophia's childish attempt to represent her as a servant.

Ever since Sara's arrival, Hermione and Sophia had done all they could to make it clear to her that she was there to work, not as a guest. Their behaviour had annoyed Nicky, and Sara had no wish to provoke a family quarrel in front of

Patrick Laird, which might happen if she retired to her room.

As the evening wore on, it was obvious to her that there was a strong, warm bond between the two men. Patrick was several years older than Nicky, and they were quite unlike brothers. Patrick was dark, much more like a Greek than Nicky was. Patrick was the taller of the two, and muscular where Nicky was lean. Nicky, although he was a very successful writer, had a diffident air about him, while Patrick oozed confidence. But there was a gentleness about him when he was talking to Nicky, almost as though he felt that his brother was a much more talented and successful person than he himself.

There was none of the sarcasm that she had noticed already. He teased Nicky affectionately, and Nicky became animated and vivacious in his half-brother's company.

Sophia, too, glowed. Her skin was flawless, her eyes luminous, her hair gleamed like fairy gold in the lamplight. Sophia was a fair-haired Greek, one of those people with large brown eyes, olive skin, and luxurious honey-coloured hair. True, she was vain and shallow—but with those looks, she didn't have to be clever, or have an attractive personality.

Only Sara and Hermione were outside the magic circle which Patrick, Sophia and Nicky had made for themselves. Once or twice Patrick tried to include his stepmother, but each time she stiffly withdrew. He and Nicky both brought Sara into the group several times, but each time Sophia brought the conversation round to their childhood, and Sara was excluded again. Once, Sophia broke into Greek. Patrick asked mildly, 'Do you speak Greek, Sara?' while Nicky snapped, 'Sophie, we speak English when guests are present!'

Sophia flashed a sulky look at Sara and remarked coolly, 'It is lucky, is it not, that I can speak English?'

'It is,' Patrick agreed. 'Otherwise, my darling, you wouldn't be able to join in our conversation,' and Nicky laughed.

'What about your work, old son?' Patrick asked at last.

'Still trying to meet deadlines. A film crew go on location in three months' time and I've to have a script ready in four weeks for them. So Sara came over from London to help me to get on with it.'

'So that's why you're here?' For the first time since they had shaken hands, Patrick looked fully at Sara.

'Of course, why else would she be here?' Sophia looked amused. 'Nikos is employing her until his work is completed.'

'I'd hardly say that,' Nicky sounded irritable. 'Sara's been invaluable to me—she's good at research, as well as being the most efficient typist I've ever known. In fact,' he looked up and smiled at her, 'I don't know what I'm going to do when the work's finished and I have no excuse to keep her with me.'

Hermione looked up from the magazine she was flicking through. Then she put it down with a sharp slap. Sophia pouted. Patrick looked keenly from Sara to Nicky, one eyebrow raised.

'You could always start writing that book you told me about years ago,' Patrick suggested.

'You will, of course, have a rest when this work is over,' Hermione said sharply. 'You should not be working now, Nikos. I say so, the doctor says so——'

'The doctor says what you tell him to say, Hermione,' her son cut in. 'To me, he says the truth. When the script is finished, I will be quite well enough to go home.'

Hermione flinched, as she always did when he referred to Britain as 'home'. In one lithe movement, Patrick got to his feet.

'Well, time I was getting back to the village.'

'But you should be staying here, with us—shouldn't he?' Nicky asked his mother.

'Nikos, we have no extra room——'

Patrick's deep voice stopped her halfhearted excuses. 'It's all right, I'm not here for very long, and old Leonie's putting me up.'

Nicky's face lit up. 'Leonie? I haven't seen her for ages. How is she?'

'As busy as ever. Get better soon, then you can come and see her for yourself. Leonie'd never come here, you know that.'

'Marina isn't——'

'Marina's in Athens. You should write to her

some time, she'd like to hear from you, I know.'
Patrick turned to his stepmother. 'Hermione, I'm
actually on the island to see you. Can we have a
word before I go?'

She looked alarmed. 'A word with me? Come
tomorrow morning, Patrick. It's late.'

He hesitated, then shrugged. 'All right, I will.'

'I'll walk to the gate with you,' Sophia said
quickly, and as they crossed the hall Sara could
hear the girl break into Greek, hear Patrick's
amused laugh and his voice murmuring a reply.

The room seemed suddenly empty without
him. Nicky went to bed, Hermione followed him
almost at once. As Sara collected the coffee cups
and washed them she heard Sophia come back
into the house and go upstairs.

A breeze toyed with the light curtains at Sara's
open bedroom window. The strong hot winds had
died down during the evening.

The room was fresh and cool, and the scent of
flowers drifted in from the garden below. She
could hear the sea, agitated by the winds, crashing
on the shingle of the private beach. Rustling from
time to time in the garden told of the nightly acti-
vities of small animals.

Sara found it difficult to sleep. Her stay on this
beautiful island had been shattered by a man who
had swept into her life like the sudden gales. And
just as the gales whipped the sea into a rest-
lessness, so had Patrick Laird left her feeling
uneasy. But why? He was no threat to her, for he

was Sophia's type of man, not hers. She was reminded, uneasily, of Richard, and yet Richard paled to insignificance beside Patrick. Neither of them were for her, she realised that only too well. She was attracted by quiet, gentle men, like Nicky.

'I don't know what I'm going to do when I've no excuse to keep her with me,' Nicky had said, an intent look in his gray eyes. Sara thumped her pillow and turned over. That was all she needed! If Nicky fell for her, his mother would be furious—and Sara would be caught in the middle.

'What are you talking about?' she asked herself suddenly, out loud. 'Why should Nicky be interested? Who do you think you are—Cleopatra?'

At last she slept, but it was a restless sleep invaded time and time again by a pirate with a mop of dark hair and clear, mocking blue eyes.

She was relieved when Nicky announced on the following morning that he wanted some of the script sent off to his agent. Sara had to travel to the nearest town to post it, taking Nicky's car. It meant that she would not be at the villa when Patrick arrived—and after the unsettling effect he had had on her, she was not eager to see him again.

After posting the manuscript, she walked round the shops and had a drink before setting back. As she neared the villa the battered Land Rover hurtled round a corner, bearing down on her. Sara had to spin the steering wheel to avoid a collision, her heart in her mouth. She sounded the horn, but Patrick Laird, angry-eyed, didn't even see her. With squealing brakes the Land Rover rounded another corner and was out of sight by the time she brought her own car to a standstill. White dust disturbed by its passing hung like a cloud in the air, then slowly settled on the bushes by the roadside.

Hermione was in a bad mood during lunch. Nicky asked her about Patrick's visit, but she merely snapped, 'It was not important!' When he tried again, she spoke angrily in Greek and he subsided, his face flushed.

Sophia, who was more often away from the villa than in it, was spending the day in Corfu Town. Sara made some attempt at conversation during lunch, but as Nicky and his mother were both sunk in their own thoughts, she gave up.

'I'm sorry about that,' said Nicky when they were in his room later. 'It can't be much fun for you when you're in the middle of a family row.'

'It wasn't a row. Your mother just didn't seem to want to talk about Patrick's visit.'

'Yes,' he frowned thoughtfully. 'Whatever it was he wanted to say to her, she wasn't pleased.'

'Neither was he.' Sara told him about her meeting with Patrick on the road. 'Why don't you ask him about it, if it's worrying you?'

But he shook his head. 'If he wants me to know, he'll tell me. I don't interfere between them. They don't get on well together, as you'll have realised for yourself. They never have. Patrick was always the rebel, and Hermione can't understand him. The ironic thing about it, and the part I don't think she can forgive him for, is that he loves Greece and the islands more than I do. He was crazy about Corfu when we were kids, and he's made lasting friends. He comes back whenever he can. But me——' he shrugged, 'I love Britain. I'm British. Hermione should have favoured Patrick— instead, she seemed to take it out on him because I was less of a Greek than he was.'

'He even looks the part,' Sara remembered her first sight of him, like a local fisherman in his shabby clothes, looking as though he belonged on the island. 'What does he do?'

'Patrick? He's an architect—a very good one. Of course, he could have taken anything on and been good at it.'

'Who's Marina?'

His head jerked round and he stared at her. 'What?'

'Marina—and Leonie. You were talking about them last night.'

'Oh—yes.' Nicky relaxed again, staring down at the pen he held between long slim fingers. 'Leonie's an old woman who lives in the village— marvellous personality. Patrick was always her favourite. And Marina's her granddaughter. We were all friends when Pat and I came over for holidays. Marina was married to Stavros, another member of the group. He—he was killed in the car crash. Do you think Patrick's attractive, Sara?'

Now it was her turn to be taken aback. 'I—I don't know. I expect so. But he's too–too brash for me.'

He raised one eyebrow, and suddenly she was reminded of his dark half-brother. 'Do you think so? That's just his way. He's a fantastic person when you get to know him—if he lets you get to know him, that is. He can be quite deep, can Patrick. I think he's looking for an anchor, someone he can identify with,' said Nicky, half to himself, staring out of the window.

'Perhaps. Now, what do you want done this afternoon?' Sara said briskly. She had had enough talk about Patrick.

Two days passed, mellow golden days as the island basked lazily in the last of the summer weather. It was early September, and the hills were smudged with smoke as the undergrowth was burned off before winter.

In a few weeks Hermione would close the villa and go to her house on the mainland. Corfu winters were wet, and she never stayed on the island later than mid-October. Nicky's script would be finished by the end of September at the latest, and he planned to leave then for Britain, though he had warned Sara not to tell his mother.

'Let her think I'm going to the mainland with her, if it keeps her happy. I don't want her to lament over the few weeks we've got left.'

Life slid back to its former routine at the village. Hermione's bad mood passed, Patrick did not reappear. Sara swam, walked, worked on Nicky's script, and resolutely put Patrick out of her mind.

She had almost succeeded when, on the third day after his appearance at the villa, a shadow fell across the notepad she was writing on. The others had all gone in Hermione's car to visit friends, and Sara had taken advantage of the silence to catch up on letter-writing, comfortably settled in the garden.

'Hard at work as usual?' said a deep, lazy, well-remembered voice. Patrick, in the same jeans but with a black open-necked shirt, sat on the flagstones by her chair.

'Trying to.'

'I won't interrupt you. I'm looking for Sophie.'

Her heart flipped. 'They're all out. I'm afraid you've had a wasted journey.'

'I never have wasted journeys. Come for a run in the Land Rover.'

'Why should I?'

'I want to talk to someone.'

'You want to talk to Sophia.'

'You'll do instead,' he said easily. 'In fact, now that I think of it, you might be better than Sophia. Come on.'

He got to his feet, but she stayed where she was.

'Well? I'm not going to coax you, girl! For

heaven's sake stop having an attack of the vapours
and come on!' he said impatiently.

'But I'm not dressed to go out——'

She had told herself, over the past two days,
that she had imagined the blueness of his gaze.
But as it raked over her, she knew that she had
been right. He took in the rose-pink blouse and
cream slacks at a glance, his eyes lingering briefly
on the blouse's deep neckline. 'You'll do. You're
not sulking because I was going to take Sophie,
are you?'

Her chin lifted and she glared up at him.
'Certainly not!'

'I like the way you say that. There's something
sharp about it—bossy. And you're far too small
and pretty to be bossy. Are you going to move, or
do I go alone?'

She flew into the villa, left a note for
Nicky, changed into practical sandals and picked
up her bag. The Land Rover was parked on a
piece of ground just outside the gate, Patrick
waiting at the open passenger door. He lifted her
up into her seat as easily as if she had been a
child.

'Where are we going?' she asked finally, as the
vehicle headed up into the hills.

'I want to show you something. I want your
opinion, and perhaps I want your support. It
depends,' he said cryptically, and lapsed into
silence, concentrating on the road.

As they headed further into the mountains, Sara

decided that the last thing she wanted to do was to concentrate on the road.

It seemed that the Land Rover was clinging to the sides of sheer precipices. One minute Sara was so close to the rock-face that she shrank back, convinced that she was going to be smeared across it like a fly caught beneath a fly-swatter; the next, Patrick's sure hands had swung the truck round a hairpin bend, and she was looking down into a valley far below. There seemed to be no room for two vehicles to pass, and yet, when they met a bus filled with cheerful, chattering people, or a car, there was always just enough room for them to pass without a tragedy.

Once, they went through a quarry, the torn rock dazzling white under the baking sun. Lorries were scattered about like toys. Patrick sounded the horn and bronzed, sweating men looked up, laughing and waving as he called to them in their own tongue.

Then he pulled the wheel round in another tight turn and they were back on the narrow road, with foliage reaching out to ensnare them, or to brush them contemptuously off the great hills where they dared to crawl.

'Breathtaking, isn't it?' His voice made her jump.

'Yes. And frightening as well.'

'Not to worry, you're safe enough. I've driven here in winter when the roadway was a river bed. Never lost a passenger yet,' he said cheerfully.

Then his face darkened. 'Or are you thinking about Nicky's accident?'

'No!' But they both knew that the denial had been too quick.

'So you heard about it. From Nicky? No—from Hermione, right?'

'Right.'

The muscle jumped in his jaw again, and his eyes were ice-blue as they watched the road ahead. 'In spite of what you heard,' said Patrick quietly, 'you're safe.'

'I know I am.'

He gave her a quick glance, then returned his gaze to the road, saying nothing. Nobody spoke until an hour had passed. Then Patrick swung the Land Rover off the track on to a broad stretch of grass, killed the engine, and said into the silence, 'We're here.'

He helped Sara down, and she stood looking around. The mountains were behind them now, and they were down near sea level. Most of the ground was under some sort of cultivation. Beyond it a small olive grove, filled with ancient, twisted trees, sloped down out of sight.

'Come on.' Patrick held out his hand, and caught her fingers in his own. Together they walked along a grassy path and entered the grove. There was nobody else about, and the trees gave welcome shade from the strength of the sun. On the opposite side of the grove Patrick stopped at a tumbledown stone wall. A small field ran down to

the beach, where waves whispered on coarse sand.
To each side stood small farms.

'What do you think of it all?'

Turning to her companion, Sara thought that
his eyes were just the same deep, strong blue as
the sea she had been looking at. 'It's beautiful—
so peaceful.'

'It all belongs to Hermione—from the foot of
that hill over there——' he indicated a spot
beyond the road—'to the beach. The farmers are
her tenants. That's what I came to see her about.
I want to buy it.'

'Why should you want it?'

'I'm going to build on it.'

She almost exclaimed with dismay, then
checked herself. She could see what a beautiful
spot this would be to live in. And if an architect
as clever as Patrick seemed to be could design the
right sort of house, the beauty of the spot might
not be lost.

As though reading her thoughts, he added, 'Not
a house for myself.'

'What else would you build here?'

'A hospital.'

Sara swung round, surprised. 'A hospital? In a
place like this?'

He misconstrued her surprise as dismay. His
eyes froze, and his brows knotted. 'I thought I
could explain things to you—but if you don't like
the idea before you've even heard it——' he
turned and began to walk back through the grove.

'Patrick! Give me a chance! At least let me know what you're talking about!'

He stopped, turned, walked back to where she sat on the wall. Various expressions flitted across his face as he looked down on her, and she realised that here was a man who was unsure of himself when it came to talking to others about things that really mattered. He had the strength, she now knew, to keep his own councel, and to only let others know what he wanted them to know.

Then he smiled, a wide grin that lit up his face, and sat down beside her. 'You're right, you should hear more about it. It just matters so much to me now that I take it for granted that everyone knows what I'm talking about. And I was right about you, too.'

'Were you?'

'I thought you might be more willing than Hermione to think things out and give a fair judgment. All right, then. I want to build a hospital—a small convalescent home really—for children from the back streets in Athens, children who don't get much of a chance to smell fresh air and run on grass, and climb trees, and—do all the things Nikos and I were able to do here as children. And this is the place. Hills, clear air, the beach, the sea, farm food and goats' milk—everything the children need!'

As he talked, his face became animated, happy, relaxed. He was talking now about something that really mattered to him, and something, the design

of the home, which was part of his work. The
mocking gleam had left his eyes, his firm, well-
shaped mouth had lost its amused twist, and
looked softer, more mobile, more——

Sara dragged her gaze away from his mouth
with an effort and gave herself a mental shake.
She was beginning to lose what he was saying, so
absorbed was she in just watching him say it.

'But why should you want to build a convalescent home for children?'

He hesitated, looked down at his hands. Then
his gaze swept up again to meet and hold hers.
'For Marina.'

There was something in the protective way he
said the name that sent a wave of pain through
Sara.

'She's the widow of a close friend of mine—
Stavros. I'm staying with her grandmother.
Stavros and Marina lived in Athens. He was a
teacher, she's a children's nurse. And they had a
dream of coming back to Corfu one day, and setting up a home for sick children. I designed it for
them over a year ago, and they were trying to find
financial backing for it. Then Stavros was killed
in the crash that injured Nikos. And I decided
that I'd like to go ahead with the home, for him
and for Marina. It's still her dream.'

'You must think a lot of her.' Sara's lips were
stiff. He nodded.

'I thought a lot of them both. I offered
Hermione a good price for the land—I wasn't

looking for it for nothing. But she won't sell. She claims that it's needed for agriculture, but I'd already talked to the farmers, and I know she's wrong. They'd be willing to let it go, for all that it is. But Hermione won't go along with anything that I'm involved in.'

'Why not ask Nicky?'

The clear blue gaze skimmed her face again.

'There are several reasons. One of them is that I won't come between Nikos and Hermione. He'd want me to get that land—he'd certainly want Marina to get the home set up. But I can't speak to him myself, because then it would be a three-way battle and no matter what happened, Nikos would suffer. He cares about his mother and about me. Hermione and I don't give a damn about each other. That's why I thought of getting Sophia on my side. She's an empty-headed little madam, but I thought I might be able to get her to use what influence she has.'

'I think Nicky's mother hopes that he'll settle down with Sophia.'

Patrick's laugh was a sound of pure amusement. 'Not a hope! He's not her type, and she's certainly not his. Nikos always had other plans, and besides, things have changed now, haven't they?

'Have they?'

He jumped up, caught at her hand again. 'Come on, I'll try to show you what the home would look like!'

He dragged her back and forth across the

ground, explaining, describing, taking time and showing great patience. And gradually, infected by his enthusiasm, she began to visualise the low, sprawling white building with its chocolate-brown shutters and its tiled, cool rooms. She saw the play area, the patio, the pool, the path down to the beach. She sensed the way the building would nestle into the palm of the land and blend without wasting the scenery. She took off her sandals and felt the grass soft and cool beneath her feet, as the children would feel it. She imagined them running along the beach, strengthening day by day, basking in the sun's heat.

'I know what you mean!' she told Patrick at last, and he smiled down at her. 'Good. I thought you might, given a chance. You'll be a better ally than Sophia. You've got a brain, and I knew I'd have to appeal to that. Whereas Sophia—well, she's all woman, and I'd have had to try to reach her emotions in the only way—well, the only way that Sophia could understand.'

Sara reddened, and he laughed, then dismissed Sophia. 'I'll show you the plans if you like—they're in Leonie's house.'

'I'd like to see them. But I have no influence with your stepmother, Patrick. She would never listen to me.'

'I know that, my love. But you have influence with Nikos. With your help, I might be able to get him interested in this scheme without getting him into direct conflict with Hermione. Get it?'

She shook her head. 'Sorry, I don't have that sort of power over him. I'm just the typist—or had you forfotten that?'

'Oh, Sara, you do underestimate yourself,' Patrick said easily. 'Come on, I've got some food in the Land Rover. It's as obvious as the neat little nose on your face that my dear brother's falling for you. All he needs is a little encouragement. You'll make the ideal couple, and you'll have more influence with him than Hermione could ever have. Hasn't he told you yet? He will—probably produce an engagement ring and everything. He's a stickler for convention, is Nikos, not like me at all. Hurry up, I'm hungry now.'

And he strode off between the olive trees, while Sara stared after him, mouth open with surprise.

CHAPTER THREE

THEY sat on the grass in the sunshine and ate bread, cheese and tomatoes. Patrick had brought along paper cups and a bottle of local wine, and as they picnicked he talked freely about the island holidays he and Nicky had spent on Corfu as children. Sara listened, fascinated.

'Have you seen a lot of the island?' he asked finally.

'Hardly anything. I've been working—and until Nicky's more mobile, there isn't anyone to go about with. I've been to Corfu Town.'

'You must see everything that you can while you're here. All work and no play, you know—I'll take you for a run some day. You should meet some of the local people too. Hermione's a snob, she only mixes with the moneyed crowd. She misses out on a lot because of that. Take old Leonie—she's the proudest, most independent person I know. She raised seven children, survived two husbands, has eighteen grandchildren and five great-grandchildren, and lives on her own, caring for a plot of land and a couple of goats. I love to stay with her when I'm here—she's got stories that never end.' Then with a disconcerting change of subject he demanded, 'Tell me about yourself.'

'There's nothing to tell.'

'So it's true—you really were manufactured and kept in a cupboard, wrapped in tissue paper, until Nicky brought you out here?'

Sara bit her lip. 'Is that the impression you get?'

'It's the impression you give. You're too perfect to be true. But——' he eyed her thoughtfully, '——there must be more to it than that. A secret lover pining for you back home?'

'Of course not!'

'You look like the sort of girl who'd attract men—so if it's not a present love, it must be a past romance.'

'No!'

'The lady doth protest too much,' he said smoothly, a laugh in his deep voice. 'Let me think—he married someone else.'

'No. He—he went away, abroad.'

'Ah! And he's not coming back.'

'Not to me,' Sara said levelly. 'Can I have more wine, please?'

The rich red liquid bubbled into the paper cup. 'You turned him down,' Patrick persisted. 'Or perhaps he never proposed. That's it! You have the air of a girl who'd want it all correct and formal. Well, there are plenty more fish in the sea of matrimony, my love.'

'Will you please——' she jumped to her feet, wine splashing from the cup and narrowly missing

Patrick as he sprawled on the grass, laughing up at her. 'If you don't stop talking like that, I'll——'

He corked the bottle and put it down in the shade. 'You'll what? Walk home?'

Looking round at the deserted countryside about them, she realised how foolish she must look. A laugh found its way to her lips, and she sat down again. 'All right, you win—I'm stuck with you!'

'Well, every story has its happy ending,' Patrick said cheerfully. 'There you were, on your own— and along came Nikos and swept you off your feet. Come to Corfu with me, he said, and you couldn't wait to follow where he led.'

'If you must know, I'm an ordinary person, doing an ordinary typing job in an ordinary agency. Nicky was one of our clients. When he was injured over here——' she could have kicked herself as she saw the muscle jump in his jaw, saw his clear eyes suddenly darken and drop to the cup in his hand. 'When he realised that he wouldn't get back to England in time to finish the film script,' she went on hurriedly, 'he contacted the agency and asked if I could come to Corfu.'

The blue eyes swept back to her face. 'He asked for you specially?'

'I usually do his work. I know what sort of assistance he needs.'

'And you want me to believe that Nikos just asked you to come to Corfu because he likes the

way you type?' The mocking smile was back.
'Come off it, Sara, you surely can't be as naïve as
that? Why do you think my dear stepmother's like
a cat on a hot tin roof? She's terrified in case you
take Nikos away from her. She's always like that
when he gets interested in a girl.'

It explained Hermione's coldness, and yet—
Sara pushed the thought from her mind with an
abrupt, 'That's nonsense!'

'He'd be a very good catch, you know. He'll
inherit a lot from Hermione. She's wealthy in her
own right. And he's doing quite well for himself
as a writer anyway. He could give you a wonderful
life.'

Anger began to well up in her at the casual note
in his voice. 'You must think that women are all
gold-diggers!'

'In my experience they are.'

'And you have such a lot of experience, haven't
you?'

The smile widened. 'Oh, a great deal.'

'Well, you've been misled. Oh, I'm quite sure
that with your looks and your charm you attract
women—a certain type of women,' she said scathingly. 'But we're not all as empty-headed as that!'

Patrick raised one eyebrow. 'What's wrong with
a woman wanting security? It's perfectly normal.'

'Not for me! I'm quite capable of running my
own life and looking after myself. I don't need a
man to look after me!'

'I'm sure you don't,' Patrick's face was crinkled

with amusement. 'But you wouldn't be averse to keeping one around, like Nikos, for enjoyment, would you?'

She sat up on the grass and glared at him. 'You're—you're——'

'They all say that, sooner or later,' murmured Patrick. In one swift movement he held her down on the soft grass, his body pinning her as she tried to struggle.

'Patrick!' she managed to say before his lips closed on hers, gently at first, then hungrily, seeking the response that, after a shocked moment, she gave him. Her mind ordered her to push him away, to turn her face from his. But at the same time her lips parted beneath his, her arms crept round him, her hands finally touched his thick dark hair. Her body throbbed to the touch of his, and she found herself reaching up for him when he lifted his head. With a short, surprised laugh he claimed her eager mouth again, claiming her as she claimed him.

The sweetness of his arms about her, the touch of his skin against her lips were sensations she had never experienced before. Then suddenly the weight of his body was gone, and she opened her eyes to see him kneeling beside her, staring down at her. With the sun behind him, she couldn't see the look in his eyes.

'Just testing,' he said a trifle huskily. 'You see, Sara—you're as willing as the next woman when a man makes a pass at you.'

He got to his feet, reached down to catch her hand, and pulled her up to stand beside him.

'I knew you weren't as untouchable as you looked,' said Patrick. The sound of the slap rang out on the still air, but he didn't even blink. He just continued to smile down at her, while the imprint of her hand reddened his tanned face.

'You really make a hobby of outraged dignity, don't you?' he asked mildly. 'I was only proving to you that women are women.'

'Even Marina?'

The smile faltered. 'Except Marina,' he said at last. 'But we weren't discussing her, were we? We were talking about you and Nikos. He's not like me—he believes in marriage and faithfulness. Much the same thing you believe in yourself, I'd imagine. He's bound to propose to you, Sara, and you should accept. He'll make you very happy— and I might get this land.'

'Why should you be so determined to marry me off to your brother?'

He began to gather up the remains of their picnic. 'Because I want the land, of course.'

'I think,' said Sara, torn between rage and humiliation, still unable to come to terms with the way he had affected her when he held her in his arms, 'I think that you're an objectionable man!'

'You're not the first to say that either, love,' said Patrick calmly. 'Come on, we've just got time to go and see Leonie and that map, if you still want to.'

He lifted her up into the Land Rover again, and they set off back up the mountains and across the top before dipping downhill once more.

Patrick whistled gently as he drove, ignoring Sara. On many of the corners they turned as they dropped back down the hills small shrines stood, colourful little dolls' houses containing flowers crammed into a jam jar or a bottle. In Corfu, Sara knew, people who survived accidents on the roads erected shrines on the spot to the saint of the day. The fact that each shrine bore witness to a life that had been spared only proved how good the local drivers were, thought Sara as the Land Rover jolted and bumped down another steep hill and through a narrow village street.

The street was a potholed lane twisting between houses that backed hard against the mountain on one side, and on the other seemed to be built out over breathtaking views of the valley far below. Pedestrians pressed themselves against the walls of the buildings as the Land Rover went through. Beyond the last house the road straightened, dropping down towards the next tight bend.

Before they reached it Patrick drew into the side and stopped the truck on a stretch of grass. Then he got down and opened the passenger door.

'Come here.' His hands were firm on her waist as she was helped down to the road. He led her further down the road, to where a retaining wall, no more than a crumbling heap of stones, divided the road from a sloping olive grove. The trees below them seemed to be trying to keep their balance on the slope, which was slight at first, then dropped sharply.

Patrick stood on a large flat stone, staring down into the valley below. 'This is where it happened,' he said abruptly.

'What happened?'

He didn't look at her. 'The accident. The accident that killed Stavros and injured Nikos. You can still see the gashes on the trees down there where the car came to rest against them.' His arm gleamed brown in the sun as he pointed to the grove. 'Well—I can still see them, anyway. Every time I come here.'

The muscle throbbed at his jawline again. The lazy, mocking Patrick had disappeared.

'It was an accident, everyone knows that!'

'Oh yes, it was an accident. A village child had been tending goats in the grove. She went across the road to pick flowers, and was going back when my new sports car came from the village. She hesitated, tried to run back—the car swerved to avoid her and went into a skid. It went off the road here, down that grassy spot below us, swung round and killed Stavros against those trees just there. Nikos was half thrown out, and his legs were trapped——'

His voice was filled with pain, and his body was tense as he looked at the trees, their scars still showing against the old bark. Sara shivered. Standing by him, under the baking sun, looking at the peaceful, empty grove, she could sense the noise of screeching metal, the dust, the child's frightened black eyes, the car ploughing its way down into the grove, ricocheting off pitted, twisted trees.

She put a hand on Patrick's arm, but he didn't seem to notice it.

'You couldn't have kept it on the road, Patrick!' She wanted desperately to ease the pain that gripped him.

He looked at her at last, his eyes darkened by despair. 'Yes, I could,' he said quietly. 'I could have kept the car on the road, and I could have saved Stavros and the child without swerving out of control. I could have done it.'

'But——'

'But I didn't, because you see, Sara, I couldn't do anything,' said Patrick, as though wrenching the words from his throat. 'Because I wasn't driving the car.'

'But Mrs Laird told me——'

'Oh, they all think that it was me at the wheel.' He turned his back on the grove, and sat down on a stone, shoulders slumped. 'But it was Nikos who was driving.'

He lifted his head, ran a hand through his hair, gave her the ghost of a smile. 'Do you know that that's the first time I've said that? Nikos was at the wheel. He wanted to try the car out. Why shouldn't I let him? He's a good driver. But it was a powerful car, and he isn't as good a driver as I am.

Sara still couldn't believe it. 'But why let you take the blame?'

'He isn't. He doesn't remember the actual accident. The last thing he remembers is leaving a friend's house, when I was driving. When he woke up in hospital he didn't even know he'd been in a car crash.'

'You took the blame for the accident? You let Nicky and his mother think that it was all your fault?'

'Why not? I was the only one who escaped unhurt. Nikos was devoted to Stavros—I couldn't visit him in hospital and tell him the truth, could I?'

'And his mother——'

Patrick brushed the air impatiently with a hand. 'Oh—her! I'm not keeping quiet for her sake. If she knew the truth she'd only say that I was at fault for letting Nikos drive. I don't care what Hermione thinks of me. I stopped caring about that years ago!'

'What about Marina?'

'She's been wonderful about it all—but then she would be,' Patrick said gently, and a pang shot through Sara at the tenderness in his voice. 'She believes that what was meant to be was meant to be. I thought of telling her, the last time I was with her—but I know I'd just be looking for forgiveness, absolution. Taking the easy way out.

After all, I should have realised that Nikos might
not be able to handle that car on the mountain
roads.'

'And realised that the little girl would appear?'
Sara asked drily. 'Surely you need to forgive
yourself, even a little.'

He shrugged, and smiled up at her again. She
was glad to see a hint of the old devil-may-care
light in his eyes.

'Maybe. It doesn't matter all that much now,
nothing can undo what happened, can it?'

'Why tell me about it?'

He looked puzzled. 'I honestly don't know.
Perhaps I just had to tell someone, perhaps I felt
that I could trust you to keep a secret. Perhaps I
feel that you've got the right to know what
happened to Nikos. I don't know.'

'Patrick, I'm so sorry!'

'For what?' he asked, and stood up quickly as
she started to speak. 'Don't answer that—we
haven't time to start talking just now. Come and
meet Leonie.'

He talked cheerfully during the rest of the trip,
and Sara felt that he was regretting the impulse
that had made him tell her the truth. She had
known about his inner strength all along, but only
now was she beginning to realise what sort of man
he was. He was prepared to carry the secret of the
accident with him for the rest of his life, no matter
what the cost to himself. She wished that she
could know Patrick as a friend—then, feeling the

touch of his lips on hers, and warmth of his arms, she realised that she could never see him as only a friend. Between them there must always be tension.

Leonie lived in a tiny house with blue shutters and a beautiful stone balustrade separating the minute front garden from the dusty lane. The small rooms were cool and uncluttered. Leonie only had as much furniture as she needed, and the floor was made of stone flags. The back door was open, an oblong of brilliant sun, framing the picture of a tiny old woman in black, grey hair tucked beneath a white headscarf, working at a patch of ground with a short-handled hoe.

She straightened slowly when Patrick called to her, and put her hoe carefully against the wall outside the door before coming into the room. As Patrick spoke in Greek, Leonie looked up at Sara, her bright black eyes missing nothing. Although her face was a mass of wrinkles, there was a youthful sparkle about those eyes, and when she smiled there was a hint of the beautiful young woman she had once been.

She wiped her hands on her black apron and took Sara's hand between her own hard warm palms as she spoke.

'Leonie can't speak English,' Patrick explained. 'She says she's pleased to meet the young lady from England.'

Gently, the old woman pushed Sara into a chair and bustled to the small stove in a corner of the room. As she prepared cups of thick black Greek coffee she and Patrick chatted to each other, obviously completely at home in each other's company. Patrick translated so that Sara could understand what was going on. Once, he laughed uproariously and said, 'She's asking if you're my lady. She thinks you'd be a very good lady for me. Don't panic—I've made it clear that we're almost strangers.'

In the flow of talk that followed, Sara heard 'Nikos' mentioned more than once, and Leonie looked at her with a new interest. Clearly Patrick had told the old woman that Sara was Nikos's 'lady'.

The only decorative piece of furniture in the room was a high dresser, polished to a magnificent shine and containing carefully hoarded china and ornaments. Several photographs stood on top of it, and Sara went to look at them as the others talked. Most of the photographs were family groups—beaming men and women surrounded by fat wide-eyed children. In the centre stood a silver-framed photograph. It was of a young couple, the man thin and dark, with a mass of hair and a lively, intelligent face. The girl also dark, and even lovelier than Sophia. She had a perfectly shaped oval face with huge smiling dark eyes and a soft, full mouth. Long dark hair framed her face, falling to below her shoulders. They looked very young, and very happy.

Sara picked the photograph up and turned to

find that Patrick was watching her. 'Is this Marina?'

He came over and took the picture from her. 'How did you know?'

'I knew she must be beautiful.'

'She's the most beautiful woman I've ever known,' he said simply. 'And that's Stavros with her.' Then he put the photograph back on the dresser. 'I'll bring the plans.'

She watched him as his broad back disappeared through the doorway into an inner room, then flushed as she realised that in her turn she was being watched closely by Leonie. The old woman smiled, said something, nodded towards the door Patrick had just gone through. He was back in a moment, and unrolled the plans on the small kitchen table.

'Come here, beside me, so that the light can shine on it from the window. Now—there's the olive grove, there's the road, there's the sea. Got it? This is where the house would have to be sited——'

Quickly, patiently, he explained it all, Leonie following it with her skinny forefinger. It was obvious that the two of them had pored over it for hours together. Under Patrick's expert guidance Sara once again began to visualise the home, this time interpreting the neat, efficient plan he had drawn out. She could see the building fitting beautifully in the hollow between the road and the grove, could see the airy rooms, the children at play, the garden with its play area for the smaller patients.

And now she could see Marina there, with the children. And—there was a lump in her throat—Patrick fitted very well in the picture, standing beside Marina, his arm about her slim shoulders.

Thinking of it, she was aware of the warmth of his arm against hers through the thin material of her shirt. At that moment he took her hand, imprisoning it in his firm clasp as he traced the outline of something on the plan with her forefinger. She stood upright, pulled her hand away, and he looked at her, puzzled.

'I should be getting back to the villa, Patrick. I've been away for hours.'

'I'll take you back,' he said quietly, but with a chill note in his voice. He released the plan and it rolled itself up so that Marina's convalescent home was hidden. There was hurt in the look that Patrick turned on her.

'Will you thank Leonie very much for her hospitality, and say that I hope to visit her again?'

He nodded stiffly, and she knew he thought that the plans had bored her.

She picked up the plan, handed it to him. 'Patrick, your design is beautiful. But I really have to get back.'

His cold blue gaze softened a little. 'Of course. I've taken up too much of your time already.'

He spoke to Leonie, who chattered back, taking both Sara's hands in hers.

'You've made a friend for life. Leonie says that you must always remember that you have a true friend in Corfu while she's here.'

On an impulse Sara bent and kissed the old lady's withered cheek, and Leonie returned the kiss warmly.

It was almost dark by the time they reached the villa gates.

'Look——' Patrick turned Sara away from the villa when he had helped her down from the passenger seat. Across the bay the last of the sun was just disappearing behind wooded slopes. Cypresses massed along the skyline like a fairy town on the horizon, complete with church spires. Half-way down the slope, on the other side of the bay, undergrowth fires glowed dully. The sky was a smooth pearl grey and the sea whispered ancient legends of the island to the stones on the beach below the villa. The air was still, as though the night was waiting for something.

'Corfu!' Patrick's voice murmured in her ear. She felt the warmth of his breath on her neck, felt his hands clasp her shoulders. 'A magic island. Anything can happen here.'

Anything. For a moment she leaned back against him, drowsily content. Then as his fingers tightened on her shoulders she was turned gently to face him. He was outlined against the grey sky, and it seemed that the first few stars to be seen were dancing in his hair. Looming over her, he looked like a Greek god, come to claim a mortal maiden.

She held her breath, like the night—waiting. But suddenly Patrick laughed, released her, brushed her cheek lightly with the back of one hand. 'All right, Sara, don't look at me as though you're convinced that I'm going to take you by force! I don't go for that. Come on, let's see if they've made the coffee!' And he flicked the gates open and headed up the short drive towards the house, leaving her to hurry after him.

Sophia and Nicky were in the lounge, and a clatter of china from the kitchen indicated where Hermione was.

Nicky's eyes lit up when Sara walked in. 'Sara, I was beginning to wonder when you'd get back!'

'I told you she'd come home eventually, Nikos,' Sophia's voice was sulky.

'Sorry, I kept her longer than I meant to,' Patrick said easily. 'We went for a drive, then we went to see Leonie.'

'Stay and have some supper, Pat.'

Patrick consulted his watch. 'No, thanks. I'm meeting a friend. I wouldn't mind some coffee, or a drink.'

'I'll do it.' Sophia drifted towards the table where bottles and glasses always stood. 'It's still the same drink, is it?' she added with emphasis, turning to survey Patrick through half-closed eyes. He returned the gaze. 'You remembered?'

Sophia picked up a bottle, reached for a glass.

'Patrick, how could I ever forget?' Her voice was low, caressing. Nicky, watching the two of them again, a little half-smile on his lips, seemed quite unconcerned.

'I'll go and help Mrs Laird,' Sara said quickly.

Without turning from the table, Sophia said, 'I think you should,' and Nicky's face hardened. Patrick, relaxed in an armchair, watching Sophia, said nothing.

'Don't tell me that we have to feed Patrick as well,' Hermione said crossly as soon as Sara went into the kitchen. She began to gather cutlery together.

'No, he's only staying for a drink.'

'Good. At least he brought you back in one piece,' Hermione's voice was malicious.

'He's a good driver.' Sara dropped a fork.

'Not good enough. My Nikos——' the Greek woman stopped, her mouth set in a thin, hard line. Her ringed fingers sliced viciously at the vegetables she was preparing for a salad.

Sara looked at the woman's plump, well-dressed figure and wished Patrick had never told her the truth about the accident. Now, she found Hermione's shallow, selfish resentment against her stepson quite unbearable.

It would have been a pleasure to have been able to wipe the complacency from the older woman's face, to have shocked her into admitting that her husband's son wasn't the wastrel she made him out to be.

'What's wrong with you tonight?' Hermione asked peevishly as Sara almost dropped another fork.

Sara swallowed hard, and smiled at her hostess. 'Sorry. I wasn't thinking about what I was doing,' she lied.

The truth, as she realised, was that in wanting so much to shake Hermione out of her complacency, Sara didn't have nearly as much strength or self-control as the man who, at that moment, was lounging comfortably in an armchair in a nearby room, laughing and talking, apparently without a care in the world.

CHAPTER FOUR

BEFORE Patrick left that evening, it was arranged that he should take Sara to explore part of the island in a few days' time.

Dismayed, she tried to argue, but Nicky himself insisted.

'It's time you saw something of the place. I've been selfish, keeping you here all the time.'

'But I'm here to work!'

'Nikos is right,' Hermione said unexpectedly. 'After all, soon you will go home, will you not?' The meaning in her deep voice was unmistakable. 'You will probably never come here again. You should see some of the island.'

'There isn't enough time, though. Not if the script is to be finished in a few weeks, Nicky.'

'Next Wednesday Hermione and Sophia and I have to spend the day with friends,' he pointed out. 'You'd be here on your own that day—might as well make the most of your leisure time. Besides, I know I can trust Patrick to take good care of you for me.'

Patrick, idly leaning against the window frame, staring out into the velvety darkness, sketched a bow. 'Indeed, sire, I'll protect the lady with my life.'

'Just as long as you drive carefully——'
Sophia's soft voice was like silk.

'Sophia!' Nicky snapped. For an instant
Patrick's smile vanished, his eyes darkened in the
way they had when he and Sara had looked at the
scarred olive trees. Then Sophia protested, 'I only
meant that everyone should drive carefully!' and
Patrick drained his glass, the smile back on his
lips as he assured her, 'I know just what you
meant—my darling! Well——' he put the glass
down and moved towards the door, 'I'd better go
back to the village and get ready.'

'Is she beautiful, Patrick?' Sophia asked.

'Of course. Aren't they always?' Patrick lifted
her elegant hand to his lips and kissed it. 'Don't
bother to get up, Nikos. I'll call for you next
Wednesday morning, Sara.'

Her hand was formally shaken, then released as
his eyes slid over her then beyond her, to where
Sophia stood.

'See you,' he said, and went out. As she looked
after him, Sophia's mouth was tight with anger.
Sara wondered again at their relationship.

She didn't have long to wait to find out. When
she emerged from the sea on the following morning, Sophia was sitting on the rocks waiting for
her. Her lithe, slender figure was a splash of
colour in a scarlet pants suit, and for a moment,
rubbing water out of her eyes, only conscious of
the colour against the white rocks, Sara thought
that Patrick was there.

Sophia's bare brown arms gleamed under the sun. She wore no make-up and her hair was pulled tightly back from her face and tied in place with a scarlet scarf. Her feet were bare, a pair of thonged sandals on the rock beside her.

'Is the water warm?' she asked in her friendliest voice, throwing a towel to Sara.

'It's beautiful. Warm and soft—you should try it.'

Sophia's fair hair swung gently as she shook her head. 'I swim only during the very hot summer. And now I prefer to swim in pools—the sea is barbaric!' she announced with a fastidious tremor of slim shoulders.

'If you lived in my country, you would appreciate the sea here.' Sara pulled off a floral bathing cap and let her hair swing loose. Sophia watched her with eyes lazily narrowed against the strong sunshine.

'Did you enjoy your trip with Patrick yesterday?'

'Very much.'

'Where did you go?'

'Over the mountains—then back to meet Leonie.' She decided against telling Sophia why Patrick had taken her out. Let him talk about Marina's convalescent home if he wanted to.

'Leonie and Patrick were always good friends. She is the grandmother of Marina——'

'I know. I saw a photograph of Marina and Stavros in Leonie's house.' The other girl's long-lashed brown eyes opened wider, flicked in her direction.

'Marina is very beautiful. That is why Patrick stays with Leonie, of course. When we were children, we were all good friends.' The Greek girl sounded absentminded, more intent on the pile of small stones she had begun to gather than on what she was saying. 'Patrick was in love with Marina.'

The sun was hot on Sara's shoulders, but she shivered slightly. 'I'm not surprised.'

'Stavros was her choice. But Patrick spent a lot of time with them in Athens. I am sure that now he would like very much to comfort Marina, to offer her more than friendship.'

If only you knew how much he was willing to do for Marina, thought Sara bleakly, remembering his determination to give her the home she wanted on Corfu, the interest blazing in his eyes as he described the building he had designed for Marina.

Sophia spread the stones out on the rock, and finally selected one. 'I am telling you this as a friend, of course,' she said finally.

'Why should you feel that you have to tell me? Warning me off?'

'Sometimes,' said Sophia vaguely, 'I do not understand the things the English say.' She turned the stone round in her pink-tipped fingers. It was of a soft grey colour, banded by shades of blue. 'I only think that you should know about Patrick. He is handsome, charming. He can be kind at times. But he amuses himself with people, and then, when he gets bored, he walks away from them. I would not want you to think, because he is kind to you, Sara, that he cares in any way about you——' every word was a drop of poison, carefully administered.

Bitch, thought Sara coolly. But even as she thought it, the poison made its mark, biting deep. She reached for her robe, put it on, forced her voice to remain impartial.

'I don't think I need to be warned, Sophia. I hardly think Patrick Laird would be at all interested in wasting his charm on me.'

The brown eyes slid over her hair, her figure, her face. 'No,' Sophia agreed. 'Patrick always had a taste for sophisticated women.

Despite herself, Sara coloured angrily. 'Even if I did come into his range,' she countered just as sweetly, 'I wouldn't be impressed by him. I prefer men who are—less obvious.'

It was Sophia's turn to colour slightly. She tossed the grey stone into the water, brushed her fingers together.

'Oh, Patrick can be most subtle when he wishes,' she stood up with the same lithe movement Patrick used. They were beautiful people, Sara thought unhappily. They belonged to a world she had never really known about. 'I know a great deal about Patrick,' the Greek girl went on, stepping daintily down from the rock and leading the way across the beach. 'He and I, we

travel a great deal. We meet, here and there—
Brussels, Paris, London. Once, a whole week in
Paris . . .' she let the words drift into the still air
between them, then turned to smile at Sara, her
eyes bright with malice. 'He can be a very
pleasant way of passing time, until one becomes
bored.'

Looking at the slim scarlet figure weaving
before her through the trees towards the garden,
Sara had to bite her lip. She knew that Sophia
was deliberately trying to annoy her, trying to
make her feel inferior, to spoil the day she was to
spend in Patrick's company. And, despite herself,
the Greek girl was succeeding. Sara had mixed
feelings about her outing with Nicky's half-
brother. Patrick annoyed her, frightened her—
and at the same time attracted her as no man had
ever done. It would be difficult enough to cope
with his presence without Sophia's words rank-
ling. She resolved, as they reached the newly-
watered garden, to put the girl's venomous conversation out of her mind as quickly as she could.

On the following day Nicky suddenly asked,
'Did you enjoy Patrick's company the other day?'

'He's quite pleasant. And I enjoyed meeting
Leonie.'

His face lit up. 'She's terrific, isn't she? I must
go and see her soon, once I'm more mobile. Of
course, she'd never come here—Leonie doesn't
approve of luxury places like this. I hope Patrick
behaved himself.'

She looked up quickly from her work.
'Behaved?'

He grinned. 'I mean—I hope he wasn't difficult. People can find it difficult to get to know
him. It's just his way, but——'

'If you mean that your brother can be down-
right insulting at times—yes, he can. But I can
take it.'

The grin broadened. 'What did he say to you?'

Her face grew warm and she turned away, fussing round the filing cabinet. 'Never mind. I told
you, I can take it.'

'I expect you can.' After a moment, he said
thoughtfully, 'On the other hand, I hope he wasn't
too nice.'

As she remembered the way Patrick had kissed
her as they lay on the soft grass after their picnic,
her flush deepened. 'Nicky, what on earth do you
mean?'

Mistaking her high colour and sharp voice for
anger, rather than confusion, he said quickly, 'I—
I'm sorry, love. I didn't mean that—oh, I think
it's just because I'm jealous.'

'Jealous? Jealous about your brother? But you
surely don't think——'.

'Jealous because I'm not fit enough to take you
out and about myself.' Nicky stared down at his
hands, avoiding her gaze. 'Jealous because I still
can't drive or walk far, because I can't take you
dancing and picnic with you among the trees, and
swim with you off the beach.'

'Oh, Nicky! Surely you know that that doesn't matter?'

He looked up now, his gray eyes intent on her face. 'It matters to me.'

'Nicky, you're getting better every day. You'll soon be able to do all those things. Look, I'll tell Patrick I can't go out with him,' she said impulsively. 'I'll wait until you and I can explore the island together. I could drive you if you wanted.'

'No, it would be silly to cancel Wednesday. I've got to go out with Hermione anyway; you'd be happier with Patrick than here on your own. And I want to take you out when I can drive again, not let you take me.' He smiled crookedly at her. 'When you're out on Wednesday, look for a nice picnic spot for us, okay?'

'I will. But remember, I'll have to go home when your script's finished.'

'Must you?'

'There won't be any reason for me to stay. And you're planning to fly back as well, aren't you?'

'Yes, but——' he caught her hand. 'Sara, let's stay on for a couple of weeks when the script's finished. We'll have a holiday. I'll pay the blasted agency if that's what you're worried about. Please?'

She hesitated, then compromised. 'We'll see how long it takes to finish the work, then decide.'

'If that's the way you want it, I'll agree. But I do want you to stay for a while. There's something I want to talk about, when I'm back to normal.'

Nicky looked up at her, that searching look again. 'Something important.'

A tremor touched her heart, and she was about to draw her fingers from his when Hermione said coolly from the doorway, 'Are you ready for lunch now, Nikos?'

Nicky took his time releasing Sara's hand, and his mother's sharp eyes missed nothing. 'Ready,' he said cheerfully. 'Give me a hand, Sara?'

'I'll help you, darling.' His mother moved quickly for a heavy woman, brushing Sara aside, leaving her to follow as the other two went across the hall, Hermione fussing round Nikos like a large and exotic butterfly round a lamp.

It seemed to Sara that the next few days flew by—and yet, in another way, the time passed slowly. Then it was Wednesday, and the villa was filled with bustle as Hermione, Sophia and Nicky prepared for their day out.

Sara hesitated over her clothes, decided a dozen times that she would stay at home, pleading a headache, the onset of a cold—anything to get out of a day with Patrick.

'Why don't I just tell him the truth—that I would rather not go?' she asked herself irritably several times. But she knew the answer. Patrick would probably brush aside her feeble excuse, pick her up under one arm, throw her into that Land Rover of his, and drive off with her.

She finally chose a sleeveless, silky tunic dress in varying shades of green with a tie belt, V-neck, and flared skirt. She slipped on a pair of comfortable open sandals and tied a green scarf loosely round her throat. Then she brushed her brown hair until it shone and tried tying it back. But the severe style which looked super on Sophia didn't suit Sara's small, neat features, and she released her hair and let it fall into a gleaming brown bell about her face. A light jacket completed the outfit.

She put on pale pink lipstick and some light perfume and went downstairs, secure in the knowledge that she was looking as fresh and pretty as she could.

At first sight of Sophia, elegantly lovely in a coffee-coloured linen trouser suit with gold jewellery and cream bag and sandals, Sara at once felt dowdy and dull. But Nicky's admiring whistle boosted her confidence a little. He looked smart in a lightweight suit instead of the shabby jeans and shirt he usually wore. The stick, and the limp, which was improving every day, gave him a distinguished air, and Sara realised for the first time, with a slight shock of surprise, that he was a very good-looking man.

An engine's roar dwindled and died outside, and after a moment Patrick strolled in through the open front door. 'All set? Not bad——' he said admiringly as he saw her standing at the foot of the stairs, then Sophia appeared from the lounge, and Patrick's eyes immediately left Sara.

'Bring some swimming things, it's too good a day to stay out of the water, there's a good girl,' he threw at Sara casually. And like a good girl, fuming under a calm exterior, she obeyed.

When she went back downstairs Hermione was marshalling her party into order. She had decided that it would be less tiring to hire a car and driver, now waiting outside.

'Have a good time,' Nicky told Sara, the intent look back as he gazed down at her.

'We will,' Patrick assured him.

'Look after her, Pat. She's important to me.'

His brother winked at him. 'I'll do that.'

'Nikos, come along! Sara, we expect to be home by ten. A light supper will do——' Hermione shooed Nicky and Sophia outside and into the car. Patrick draped an arm casually across Sara's shoulders as they stood on the steps watching the car move off. He laughed as she moved aside, out of his embrace. As the car drove off, Hermione waved a stubby, jewelled hand regally, Nicky turned to smile at Sara, and Sophia's lovely face swam behind the glass as she stared straight ahead, ignoring the couple standing on the steps. If the friendly embrace was meant to annoy Sophia, Sara thought with wry amusement, it had not succeeded.

'Hermione always manages to make a visit look like a charabanc outing to Blackpool,' her stepson observed uncharitably. 'Ready, then?'

To her surprise, the Land Rover was not hulking in the layby outside the gate. Instead, a glossy blue open car waited for them.

'Like it? I only use the Land Rover for everyday jaunts. This is the real love of my life. Put that scarf over your hair—it'll be breezy when we get going.' He helped her in and switched on the engine. A deep-throated rich purr came from beneath the bonnet, and Patrick turned to Sara, eyebrows raised.

'Scared to trust yourself in this car with me?'

When she shook her head, the devil-may-care grin lit his face. 'Good girl! Right, here we go.' And the car glided on to the roadway and accelerated swiftly and smoothly as Patrick settled in his seat.

He was an excellent driver. Although they were travelling at speed, Sara felt completely confident with him. His hands nursed the wheel with a sure touch, his face was calm and absorbed as he watched the road. It was as though he and the car were one entity, completely in harmony. She could well believe that, had he been at the wheel on the day of the accident, Stavros would be alive and Nicky would not be walking with the aid of a stick. And she herself would be in England, working in some office, instead of racing through this beautiful island, Patrick at her side. For a moment, she selfishly felt glad that she was there, with him.

The car soared up the mountain roads like a bird. It slipped in and out of the little villages, easing itself along narrow streets then developing its contented purr as it regained the open road. The wind snatched at Sara's scarf, and she refastened it a few times, then gave up and pulled it off, letting her hair whip across her face.

Patrick's white teeth showed in a smile of approval as he glanced at her. He started to sing in a deep, surprisingly good voice; a Greek song, the words blown away to tumble in the dust of the road behind them.

'Look!' Sara touched his arm and he slowed the car slightly. They were passing a wooded slope on which was built a small white platform, pillared and roofed like a miniature temple. A pile of hay had been placed on the platform, which was a few feet from the ground, and a solitary brown and white cow stood with its neck stretched between two pillars, chewing contentedly at the hay.

'It could only happen in Corfu!' Patrick shouted as the car accelerated.

'Why would a temple be in the wood?'

'Somebody must have thought it was a good idea—or somebody thinks his cow deserves special treatment.'

'Perhaps we imagined it all. Patrick, turn back and let me see it again!'

But he shook his head, his dark hair ruffled in the wind. 'No—I told you this was a magic island. You don't get a second chance—everything might fall to dust if you tried it!'

The car turned off the road and dipped down a twisting lane that was almost vertical in places. The land ended in a path near the water's edge, within sight of a village consisting of a taverna, three houses, and a cluster of fishing boats and pleasure boats riding the calm waters of the harbour.

Patrick parked the car. 'Time for a drink.'

They drank ice-cold lemonade, sitting on a terrace overlooking the sea. The misty mass of the Greek mainland was in sight across the water. The daughter of the taverna owners, a lovely little blonde girl about three years old, sat at the next table chewing an apple and swinging her brown legs as she stared solemnly at the visitors. She giggled when Patrick teased her, and answered him in a clear, high voice.

Then they walked round the harbour and sat on the sea wall. On one side the white-topped waves broke, on the other, before them as they sat there, the harbour was like a dark mirror, the water so clear that the brightly-coloured little boats seemed to be moored in mid-air. Beyond the harbour magnificent cypresses marched from the summit of the hill to the edge of the water, to be mirrored in its stillness.

'It's—incredible,' Sara said at last.

'You haven't seen Paleokastritsa yet. Now, that's heaven on earth,' Patrick assured her. A breeze gently lifted his hair as he turned to watch a man at work on his boat. In that setting, dressed

as he was in white shirt and black trousers and
safari jacket, he looked more like a pirate than
ever.

'I can't think why Nicky prefers to live in
London, when he could live here,' commented
Sara.

'That's probably the answer—he can come here
whenever he wants. Nikos doesn't love Corfu as
much as I do—I knew from the first moment I
saw it that it would be important to me.'

'You travel a lot, don't you? Rome—Paris——'

He turned back to her, the eyebrow lifted.
'Who's been talking about me? Yes, I travel. But
I always come back here.'

'Do you have a base anywhere?'

'No. I'll build myself a house here, some day
when I get the urge to settle down. It depends on
the times.'

'The times?'

'A time to work, a time to worry, a time to grow,
a time to stop—I read a poem about the times
once. It stuck in my mind. I live by the times. A
time to have fun—that's what I'm in now.'

'What about a time to care?'

A smile twisted his mouth. 'You think I don't
care enough?'

'About some things. About Nikos, and not
wanting him to know the truth about himself.'

Patrick stood up abruptly. 'Nikos is special. He
always has been. And talking of times, it's time
we were on our way before we're invaded.' He

nodded at a glass-sided pleasure boat that was anchoring across the harbour. Its load of holiday-makers stepped ashore gingerly and began the climb from the water to the taverna above, calling to each other. Their voices floated across the harbour, disturbing the peace of the place.

'Germans,' Patrick commented. By the time they had made their way back round the harbour the tourists had settled like a flock of brightly-coloured birds at the taverna's tables. Patrick called out a farewell to the proprietor and his wife as they passed on their way to the car, and Sara saw that some of the younger women from the boat—and some of the older women too—looked at her companion with interest.

She studied him as he opened the car door for her and then went round to the driver's door. Although his jacket hung open and his shirt was unbuttoned to show an expanse of smooth brown chest, he looked casually elegant. He wore clothes well, moved with a panther's grace. She wondered what he looked like in the city, when he was working. Somehow she couldn't quite imagine him in a collar and tie.

'What are you staring at me like that for? Have I grown an extra head?'

'I was wondering what you look like when you're all dressed up,' she said without thinking, then blushed.

'Devastating. You must invite me out some time and see for yourself,' said Patrick, swinging into the bucket seat beside her. 'Hold on, I've got to take this thing up to the road backwards. No room to turn. Enjoying yourself?'

She was. More than she thought she would. More, she realised guiltily, than Nicky would like.

CHAPTER FIVE

PALEOKASTRITSA was indeed breathtakingly beautiful, a small town built on a bay of placid blue-green water, encircled high, wooded headlands and guarded by rocks that thrust themselves out of the water between the cliffs.

They arrived in time for a swim before lunch, and Patrick took Sara to a smaller bay separated from the main bay by a small stretch of land.

Here were rocks where they could change into bathing costumes, and coarse sand with several people stretched out, sunbathing. A number of the women were topless, and when Sara joined him Patrick looked her over in a studied manner, then raised his eyebrows.

'The whole bikini today? Not fashionable on this beach, love.'

'I'd rather wear it all.'

'I seem to remember——'

'And I wish you'd forget!' She brushed past him and headed for the water, ignoring his murmured, 'Once seen . . .' as he followed her.

He swam as he drove—as though he had been born to it. His muscular brown body drove through the water, and he had soon left her behind. Sara was content to take her time, feeling the sea's cool silken touch, resting on her back now and then to gaze up at the flawless blue sky, turning over to swim again, her face in the water so that she could watch the submerged rocks and sand slip by beneath her.

Patrick swam back to her. 'Race you to that rock out there.'

She trod water, shaking her head. 'I'm not in the mood for racing. I just want to enjoy the water.'

With a flick of his head he started out towards the rock as she watched. He had an athletic body, broad-shouldered, slim-hipped, with long, powerful legs. For the first time in her life she found herself assessing and admiring a man's body. Well, why not—hadn't Patrick openly studied hers? Richard was well built, but she always had a sneaking feeling, seeing him in trunks, that he would one day run to fat. There seemed to be no chance of that with Patrick.

She began to swim towards the rock he had pointed out. For a moment she saw his dark head against the light stone, then he dropped back into the water and disappeared. She stopped, treading water, looking for him. Then she yelped and almost choked on a mouthful of salty water as hands touched her thighs, slid up to shape her hips and curve round her waist, up again to cup gently over her breasts.

'Sorry,' said Patrick from behind her. 'Didn't realise I'd blundered into you.' But there was a chuckle deep in his voice and he held her body against his for a long moment, his fingers moving teasingly along the line of her bikini top, before he released her.

After their swim, they stretched out on the sand and let the sun dry them. Sara drifted in a pleasant golden haze, eyes closed, face upturned to the sky. When a shadow darkened her lids she lifted them to see Patrick bending over her, his face close to hers.

'I'm starving—and you're almost asleep.'

'Just relaxing.' She stretched luxuriously, then suddenly realised how close he was, his blue eyes travelling over her face, her throat, her shoulders.

'I'll go and get dress——' she scrambled awkwardly to her feet. He caught at her hand, rising with her in that single, easy movement of his. 'Not so fast. You're all sandy. I'll brush it off for you.'

His hands, moving slowly over her back, made her tingle, shiver slightly.

'Cold?' said Patrick in her ear.

'Just—someone walking over my grave, I expect.' The touch of his fingers was almost unbearable. 'Surely all the sand's off by now?'

There was a lazy, intimate drawl in his voice. 'Ages ago. You want me to stop?'

'Oh—Patrick?' She caught up her towel and her clothes and started for the rocks.

'Hey, what about me?' he called after her. She turned, went back, began to brush the grains of sand off his broad, smooth brown back.

'You've got a lovely touch,' he said over his shoulder. 'I expect a lot of men have told you that.'

'More than I can remember.' The tingle that his touch had aroused in her was still there as she ran her hands over his skin, but he didn't seem to notice.

They ate at one of the tavernas crowding the main bay, then walked up the steep road that led to the monastery, hidden high on one of the headlands, surrounded by trees and overlooking the sea.

Although it was filled with tourists, the monastery bore an air of uninterrupted peace. Together Sara and Patrick wandered round the courtyard with its bell tower and its well, explored the tiny colourful garden, looked through the precious icons, visited the small shop, and leaned on the protecting wall, looking down to where the town was spread out far below. In the bay, rocks were deep blue beneath the water, the same colour as Patrick's eyes. Swimmers, from that height, looked like water beetles, their limbs clearly seen in the water.

'Now I know why I had to come here,' said Sara as they started down to the town. 'It's hard to believe that all this is real.'

'It's real. Nature is the best architect of all. And as far as I'm concerned, she was at her peak when she designed Corfu. When I'm elsewhere,' said Patrick thoughtfully, stopping to admire the view again, 'I like to think that this is part of the world. And it always will be. In all its perfection.'

'I hope I'll be able to come back again, one day.'

'No problem. Marry Nikos, and you can come back as often as you like.'

'Patrick——'

'Hasn't he asked you yet?' When she didn't answer, he said, 'He will. He'll pop the question before you type "The End" on that manuscript of his, you'll see. Now I'm going to take you to see the blue caves.'

'You mean there's more to see?'

There was. They hired a small boat, complete with boatman, and set off across the bay towards the fringe of light-coloured rocks.

'Aren't you bored? You must have seen it all hundreds of times.'

'I could never get bored with Corfu. Besides, I'm enjoying it all over again with you.' Patrick draped an arm across her shoulders, so that his fingers brushed her bare arm as the boat moved. He pulled her closer to him as the boat slowed and nosed into the first cave.

'It's all right, the boatmen here are very romantic,' he said with a laugh as he felt her stiffen. 'This man would be most disappointed if he didn't think we were sweethearts.'

Sara thought of moving away—then as they moved from the sunlight into the cave she forgot all about what the boatman thought. Her eyes

were wide as she looked at the cave—filled with a
clear blue light that turned the drops of water to
sapphires as they fell back from the boatman's
oar.

With Patrick's arm about her, she leaned over
the side and trailed her fingers in the heavenly
blue water, lifted a handful of drops and watched
them thread through her grasp like jewels. She
had never seen anything as lovely.

In the cool blue of the caves Patrick's eyes
blazed, dominating his brown face, holding her
own gaze when she turned to look at him, so that
she turned away quickly, afraid to look into their
depths for too long, afraid of what she might see—
or might not see.

Evening was on its way by the time they drove
out of the town. The sun dipped in the sky, and
as they reached the countryside they passed vil-
lagers bringing their precious animals in from the
fields. Some of the sheep and goats were led along
on cords, and most of the old women who tended
them carried bundles of firewood strapped to their
backs.

A priest passed, a dignified figure riding
placidly on a small, patient donkey. Two bare-
footed children coaxed an obstinate goat towards
home. Everyone had time to stop and look at the
car as it passed, some waving, others merely
watching it solemnly.

'Hungry?'

'Yes.'

'I'm taking you to meet friends of mine, Andreas and Nina. They run a taverna with a guesthouse above it. Do you like Greek dancing?.
'I love it. But I can't dance. Can you?'
Not as well as Andreas. We'll be there in half an hour.'

The taverna was low-ceilinged, smoky, and filled with people. Greek, German and English voices could be heard as they approached the open door. The voices mingled with loud Greek music played on a record player behind the tiny bar.

Patrick was welcomed with open arms by Andreas and Nina, a handsome middle-aged couple brimming with energy and cheerfulness. A full-scale party seemed to be in progress, though Patrick explained as seats were found for them at a table that it was the same every night, no matter who was there. The islanders loved company, and language was no barrier.

A bottle of wine and two glasses appeared before them, and after a long and noisy discussion with Patrick, Andreas disappeared into the small kitchen behind the bar. In a surprisingly short time he reappeared with plates of fish and shishkebabs. It was the best meal Sara had ever eaten. The usual delicious Greek salad accompanied the dishes. Andreas and Nina sat at their table, jumping up every now and then to attend to another guest. Neither of them spoke English, but Sara found it quite easy to understand what they wanted to say to her. With the noise in the taverna, ordinary language would have been impossible.

Patrick laughed and talked, completely at home. Later, when everyone had eaten and the customers were lingering over their wine, Andreas began to dance, bringing some tourists on to the floor with him, teaching them the basic steps patiently.

Then Andreas put on another record, announced, 'Thees—men only!' and signalled to Patrick, who jumped to his feet.

The dance was beautiful, filled with intricate steps that wove a graceful pattern. For all his bulk, Andreas danced well, and Sara was impressed at the way Patrick's feet seemed to flow effortlessly from one step to another. The men danced as partners, yet without touching, each seeming to know instinctively what the next move was. They were applauded loudly at the end, then the tempo changed with the next record, and Patrick whisked Sara from her seat.

'Come on—time to work for your dinner!'

'But I don't know how to dance this stuff!' she appealed, but he laughed down at her.

'Stay with me, and listen to the music. You'll be all right.'

His hand was firm on her shoulder, guiding her. As she listened to the music, she found that there was a pattern that her feet wanted to follow.

By the time the record ended, she had begun to feel the beat of the music in her blood, had begun to understand some of the graceful steps. She stayed on the tiny dance floor, kicking her sandals off so that she could move more easily, gaining confidence as each dance came and went.

'You're not bad,' Patrick grinned down at her, and she laughed, pushing the hair back from her flushed face.

'I had no idea how wonderful it was! What's this one?'

The tempo was new to her. He reached out to her throat and plucked the green scarf off.

'A kerchief dance. It's a courting dance—in the old days they weren't permitted to hold hands, so they each held one end of a kerchief. Like this——'

One end of the scarf in her hand, Sara followed him through the dance. The beat was slower, sensuous. In a dream, she moved around the small floor beside Patrick, close, but not touching, turning beneath his outstretched arm, following him, moving back from him. She forgot about the crowded taverna, the smoke from the cigarettes that all Greek men seemed to chain-smoke. There was only the two of them, the music, the dance, and the scarf—a lifeline that she mustn't let go, because if she did she might lose Patrick.

When the music stopped she looked round, dazed, and discovered that they were the only couple on the floor.

'Bravo!' Andreas led the applause, laughing, shouting something to Patrick, who smiled in reply. Then he looked back at Sara, gazing down at her, his eyes holding hers.

A British pop song was put on the record player, and people got up to dance. Slowly, Patrick put the scarf round Sara's throat again and tied it. Then he led her to the table and poured out some wine for them both. The spell was broken, but she still felt stunned by the intensity of the dance.

'You danced that well,' he said at last, conversationally. She took her glass, sipped the wine.

'It's—interesting.'

'They weren't allowed to touch, but they were allowed to dream. They had to find some way to let each other know how much they wanted to be closer.' His eyes drifted over her face, her hair. The music changed to a dreamy tempo and he stood up. Sara slipped into his arms, her head on his shoulder, as they moved across the small floor, unspeaking.

'I think I'm under a spell,' she said when the music had ended. 'You're right—this is a magic island.'

He looked deep into her eyes. 'You have to be the right sort of person to feel the magic, though. Once you do, the island will never let you go. Never.'

The night was velvety when they left the taverna. Patrick drove slowly, the headlamps cutting through the dark and picking up jewelled lights from the eyes of small animals by the side of the road.

They didn't speak until the engine shut down outside the villa.

'Home again, Princess,' he said softly into the silence. 'The day's over.'

'What time is it?'

He moved in the darkness beside her, and she saw the brief glow of a watch dial. 'Just after midnight.'

'After midnight!' She sat upright, shocked.

'And you haven't turned into a pumpkin after all!' he teased, but she was too busy getting out of the car to pay any attention. Patrick caught up with her as she opened the gate and hurried down the drive.

'No lights on—they must all be in bed! And I said I'd have supper ready when they got back!'

They were speaking in whispers, and his lips brushed her hair as he bent to talk to her. 'Sara, my love, it wouldn't hurt them to get supper themselves. Stop fussing and ask me in for a cup of coffee.'

'It's very late, and Mrs Laird's probably furious with me as it is——' She fumbled for her key, found it, and opened the door.

'All right,' said Patrick cheerfully, his voice loud in the night, 'I'll just stay out here and serenade you——'

'No! Come in, then, but for goodness' sake be quiet!' she hissed, and he slipped through the door after her and closed it quietly.

'Don't put the light on—you'll disturb Nicky!'
She took his hand and led him through the hall to
the kitchen, where she switched on the light. They
blinked at each other in the sudden brilliance.

'After all that bother, I need a coffee,' Patrick
whispered reproachfully. Sara filled the kettle and
was putting cups out when the phone shrilled. She
jumped and dropped a cup. Patrick, sitting at the
kitchen table, caught it on the way down.

'Nervy, aren't you? Go and answer that and I'll
see to the coffee.'

'Sara? Where have you been? I've been trying
to get through for ages!' Nicky's voice was sharp
with anxiety.

'Nicky! Where are you——!' Foolishly, she
turned to stare at his closed bedroom door. Patrick
appeared in the kitchen doorway, a shadow
against the light, leaning on the frame with arms
folded.

'I thought something terrible had happened to
you, Sara!'

She heard the tension in his voice, realised with
a mixture of compassion and anger that Hermione
had no doubt made much of her disappearance,
her safety in Patrick's car.

'We stayed out later than I intended to, that's
all. Patrick took me to visit some friends of his,
and we danced for a while.'

'Oh.' It was impossible to tell what he meant
by that flat comment. 'Look, Sara, the blasted
hired car broke down, and by the time we found

out that it wasn't coming for us, it was too late to start making other arrangements. We're going to stay here overnight and come back in the morning.'

'I see,' she said carefully.

'Is Patrick there?'

She looked at the tall figure in the doorway.

'No.'

'He could have taken you to a hotel for the night. I don't like the thought of you being on your own, darling.'

'I'll be perfectly all right, really.'

'If you're sure——' he sounded unhappy. 'Well, I'll be back as soon as I can in the morning. Take care. I'll miss you.'

When she had hung up she stared at the phone, sitting smugly on the table. Why had she lied about Patrick? She knew perfectly well that it was because Sophia or Hermione, or perhaps Nicky himself, would have read something into it if she had said that Patrick was still with her. And there had been something different about Nicky's voice——

'Do you mean,' said Patrick's voice plaintively, 'That I've been dodging about here in the dark and whispering like an idiot—in an empty house?'

'Hmmm?'

'I gather that that was Nikos. If he phoned, he can't be asleep in that room over there. And no doubt wherever he is, Sophie and Hermione are still with him. The house is empty, not asleep.'

She switched on the hall light. 'How was I to know that the hired car had broken down? They're staying where they are overnight.'

'Well, it means that we can enjoy our coffee in comfort, instead of whispering like conspirators in the kitchen.' Patrick went into the lounge and switched on a lamp, then reappeared in the doorway, records in his hands. 'We can have music as well. What would you like, Princess?'

'It doesn't matter.'

'Okay. Kettle's boiling.'

When Sara carried the tray of coffee in, he was sprawled comfortably in a chair, head back, eyes closed. Soft music filled the room. Sara poured out coffee and settled on the sofa opposite Patrick, watching him, marvelling over how vulnerable he looked. Then his eyes snapped open and their blue light animated his entire face once more.

'Have you spoken to Nikos about the land?' He helped himself to sugar, the spoon tiny in his large hand.

'I'm waiting for the right time,' she said evasively.

'I don't have a lot of time myself, love. I've to be in Brazil in four weeks' time, and I'd like to know where things stand before I go. It might take a while for Nikos to sweeten his mama once he's agreed to the idea.'

'This children's home—it's very important to you, isn't it?'

'It's needed, and it's a sound idea. I'm offering Hermione a good price, and I'd like to start work as soon as the winter rains are over. The first children could be in by next yeat at this time. And I'd like an excuse to get Marina back home, now that she's on her own.'

Sara moved uncomfortably on the sofa, put her coffee cup down. 'Why doesn't she come back anyway?'

He looked at her, not really seeing her. 'She's independent. She needed to be among strangers for a little while, to get used to the idea of life without Stavros. And she's dedicated. She'll stay in Athens, nursing, until I can give her a good reason to come back to Corfu. A reason like supervising the building of the home.'

'You must care a great deal about Marina,' she said bleakly, and he glanced quickly at her, then down at his hands.

'I care about a lot of things, and a lot of people.'

'I still don't think that I've got much influence with Nicky.'

Now he looked full at her, impatience in his look, his voice. 'Then work on it. Persuade him. For goodness' sake, girl, you surely don't need lessons from me on how to charm a man!'

'I've never been outstandingly good at it.'

He laughed. 'That old flame of yours? Forget him. He was the non-marrying kind, like me. Nikos is different. I promise you that he wants to

marry you. He has that look in his eye. You'll
know where you are with Nikos. And where you'll
be with Nikos, eventually——' his eyes swept over
her again, '——is in a church, with you in orange
blossom and virgin white, and Hermione sniffling
into a black-bordered handkerchief.'

Sara leaned forward and poured out more
coffee. 'You make it all sound so attractive,' she
said acidly.

'What could be better? You get Nikos and
Corfu, he gets you, I get the land, Marina gets
her children's home. Are you sure Nikos hasn't
even hinted yet? He's being very slow.'

She finished her coffee swiftly and put the cup
back in its saucer with a clatter. 'Patrick, thank
you for a wonderful day, but it's late, and I'm
tired, so if you don't mind——?'

'Yes?' He stayed where he was, smiling up at
her as she stood over him.

'Patrick, go home.'

'You're throwing me out?'

'Something like that.'

'And you're going to stay here all night, all
alone?'

'I'm not a child.'

The blue eyes wandered over her, lingering
here and there.

'I can see that,' he said solemnly.

'And I can take care of myself!'

'No doubt you can, my love. But I couldn't
allow it. I'm responsible for you, remember? I

promised Nikos that I would take good care of
you.'

'Patrick, please——'

'So naturally,' drawled Patrick, 'I care about
your wellbeing. That's why I'm going to spend
the night here, with you.'

CHAPTER SIX

'PATRICK, for the last time, you can't stay here tonight!' Sara was exasperated, Patrick unruffled.

'Why not?'

'Because we'd be alone!'

'That's what I'm thinking about. Really, Sara, you're a little prude at times. You didn't tell Nikos that I was with you when he phoned, did you? Why not?'

She sank on to the sofa, struggling to find the right words.

'You kept quiet because you thought he might not like to think of us together, in this empty house? Or was it because what he doesn't know won't hurt him?' Patrick's voice was silky. 'Quite right, my love. Who's to know? I'll be gone early in the morning. The perfect end to a perfect day——'

Before she could move he had left his chair and was sitting beside her, one finger trailing gently, caressingly down her arm.

'Leonie will expect you back tonight!'

He smiled, moved closer. 'She knows that I'm old enough to take care of myself. She won't worry.' His hand left her arm, moved up to entangle itself in the hair at the nape of her neck.

'Stop fussing, Sara, let's enjoy the rest of the night——'

She pulled away and got to her feet, glaring down at him.

'So you make a habit of being out all night, do you?'

He shrugged. 'I'm old enough. And so are you. How old are you?'

'Twenty.'

'And I'm thirty-three, so we're both adults. You don't have to behave like a prim fourteen-year-old,' he admonished her gently. 'You can do what you like now, you know.'

'Not,' said Sara furiously, 'with you!' And yelped as steel fingers caught at her wrist and whipped her on to the sofa. Before she could sit up, Patrick's weight was pinning her down, his lips seeking hers, his hands moving over her.

'Do you know your trouble, love?' he asked breathlessly when he finally sat up and let her gasp for air, 'It's not that you don't like men. Your trouble is that you'd love to be made love to—you want it very much. But you're afraid to admit it.'

Then his fingers gripped her wrist cruelly again. 'Sorry, I don't let anyone slap my face twice. You've already had your turn.'

She stayed where she was, afraid to get up, nursing her aching wrist. 'If you don't go away, I'll tell Nicky!'

'Tell him what?' He looked her over deliberately, leaning back against the arm of the sofa. 'You should see yourself, flushed and starry-eyed and tousled. You can be quite beautiful when you're aroused, Sara. And you're aroused now.'

It was true. Her body felt as though it was on fire, her lips tingled from the touch of his mouth.

'Sophia warned me about you!'

His well-shaped dark eyebrows lifted lazily. 'Did she? So she thought you needed warning? I wonder why? And what did that lovely branch of poison-ivy tell you about me?'

'That you amused yourself with women and then walked away from them.'

'What's wrong with that? I amuse them as well. I never get complaints——' He reached for her again, but this time she managed to get to her feet, backing away warily. He stayed where he was, watching her, that maddening smile quirking the corners of his mouth.

'All right, Patrick, perhaps I am frigid, by your way of it. Perhaps I'm only an object of amusement to you. Perhaps making love to me would pass a few dull hours. But as far as I'm concerned,' she said scathingly, 'I'm not interested in Sophia's cast-offs. So you might as well go and leave me here alone. I doubt if anything worse than you can happen to me tonight!'

The words had their effect. His smile disappeared, anger lanced into his eyes. 'Cast-off? What has that little bitch been telling you?'

She pressed her attack forward, determined now to hurt him as much as she could. 'She said that you'd spent a week in Paris together, that you amused her when she was bored. Then you became a bore too.'

His reaction startled her. For a moment he stared, then he threw back his head and laughed, peals of pure mirth rolling round the room.

'That is really good, coming from Sophie!' He gasped, when he could speak. 'And you believed her?'

'Why not?'

'My dear girl, you're so naïve it's a wonder you were ever allowed out by yourself! Listen— Sophie is an empty-headed little—well, she's neither naïve nor frigid, let's just put it that way. She has a lovely face, and an exciting body, and a pin-brain. Attracting men is all Sophie is interested in, and any man who doesn't fall at her feet and swear undying passion brings out the venom. I didn't fall into line, and she still hasn't forgiven me.'

Sara sat on the armchair. 'You mean, she was just an interlude with you?'

He looked thoughtfully at her. 'If you want to know the truth about that week in Paris, you're going to be disappointed. I don't have to account to you for my life. I'm a free agent, I live as I choose. And I didn't choose Sophie, which is all that need concern you. Now, we'll wash the coffee cups, shall we?'

They washed the cups in silence. Sara stole a look at Patrick's face now and then, but his expression was impassive, giving nothing away. When the kitchen was neat and everything put away, he eyed her levelly, hands on hips.

'Before you start screaming hysterically again, I'd better explain that I'm going to spend the night in Nikos's room. I'm responsible for you, and I'm not leaving you in this house on your own tonight. Any objections? No? You can lock your door if you like.'

She felt like a child that had behaved badly, and had been dismissed. Upstairs she had a warm shower, then got into bed. But she couldn't sleep.

The events of the day flashed through her mind again and again. Patrick's hair dark against the white sun-splashed walls of the little monastery. Patrick in the water. Patrick's arms about her as they danced in the taverna—the dreamy look in his eyes as he guided her through the kerchief dance.

Patrick—Patrick—Patrick! His presence down-stairs seemed to fill the whole house. Once, she thought that she heard a door closing, but when she sat upright, straining her ears in the night's silence, there was nothing to be heard. She lay down again and remembered the gentleness in his voice when he mentioned Marina. It must, she thought, take a very special person to capture Patrick's heart as Marina had captured it.

Finally she got up and went over to the window, then back to her mirror, where her face swam like a waterlily in the darkness of the room. She brushed her hair slowly, hoping to lull herself into drowsiness.

Something clattered on to the floor downstairs, and she stared at her night-self in the mirror. There was a scrabbling sound from the hall below, and she remembered that she hadn't bothered to check the window shutters and the front door before going to bed. It could be an intruder, or an animal that had got in through an open window. Suddenly, as she pulled on a light dressing-gown and opened the bedroom door, she was glad that Patrick was in the house.

She went down the stairs on silent bare feet, reached for the light switch, and clicked it on.

Patrick, standing by the front door, screwed his eyes up against the light. He wore jeans, and was naked from the waist up. His feet were bare, and a damp towel trailed from one hand. A small table lay on the floor beside him, the ornament that normally stood on it lying on the tiles some distance away.

'I didn't manage to find my way across the hall in the dark,' he said at last, staring at her as she stood at the foot of the stairs. 'I didn't have you to guide me.'

'What on earth are you doing?'

He bent to pick up the ornament, replace the

table. The towel dropped to the floor. 'I went down for a quick swim. I couldn't sleep.'

'Neither could I.'

'Oh.' Now she could see drops of water in his hair, reflecting the light like jewels. He looked again like a Greek god, and she found it difficult to take her eyes off him.

'I'll find my way back to Nikos's room now,' he said in a husky voice, and when she didn't move he went on 'Sara, put the light out and go back to bed, for goodness' sake! Don't stand there and look at me like that. I'm supposed to be looking after you for my brother.'

'I can look after myself.' The hall was warm enough, but she was shivering.

'Can you, Sara?' the whispered words spanned the space between them. As she waited for him he crossed to the stairs, his feet slapping gently on the tiles.

Gently, Patrick reached out and cupped her face in one hand. Then the hand moved over her neck to her shoulder. As he pulled her towards him, Sara flipped the light switch off.

His skin was silky and cool to her touch, damp and salty under her lips. His lips drifted tantalisingly over her face, and salt water from his hair brushed her cheek as he bent to kiss the hollow of her throat. Then he lifted his head and, at last, kissed her on the mouth—first, a probing, questioning kiss, and then, as her lips parted beneath his, a passionate kiss that fanned her body into a blaze of longing.

It seemed that she had been waiting all her life for this man, this awakening. With a long shuddering sigh she relaxed against him, and he echoed the sigh as he held her tight with one arm, his free hand twisting in her hair, pulling her head back so that he could kiss her again hungrily, triumphantly.

'You're not a dream after all——' he half murmured, half groaned into her neck. 'You're a woman, Sara!' And when she stopped his words with her fingers, his teeth bit into her thumb.

Her dressing gown whispered to the floor, and Patrick picked her up with one easy movement, murmuring 'Now, let's hope I don't drop you in the dark!'

Sara laughed into his shoulder, her arms about him, her palms lovingly shaping themselves to his back as he carried her across the hall, through a door. Then he put her down, and she reached up and pulled him close again.

The straps of her nightdress were pushed aside impatiently, the soft material falling to her waist as his lips traced a path of fire from her throat to her shoulder, and from there to the curve of her breast.

Her hands explored his body as eagerly as his hands explored hers. Their passion was mutual, their longing for each other shared.

'Sara——' Patrick groaned in the darkness, and

she turned to hold him as he moved to lie beside her. Her face nestled into a pillow, and as well as the sea-scent of Patrick's body she sensed another faint perfume. It nagged at her memory even as she gave herself to Patrick's caresses, nagged until she identified it as the after-shave that Nicky used.

Nicky! Her eyes snapped open, and she twisted to look beyond Patrick's shoulder. Dark objects outlined against the dull light from the window identified themselves as a filing cabinet, a type-writer. She was in Nicky's room, lying on his bed, making love with his brother——

'Patrick!'

'What is it?' His voice was gentle, thick with longing. Sophia and Marina belonged to another world—for this moment, in the soft, shielding darkness, Patrick was hers. But even while her body craved to be completely possessed by him, her mind was rebelling. She pushed him away, tried to sit up. 'Patrick—not here!'

He didn't understand. His weight held her down, his hands demanded their right. But she insisted, until he lifted his head, his body tense beside hers.

'Not here—not in Nicky's room!'

There was a long silence, then the night air was cool on her body as Patrick left her and stood up.

'Trust you to remember your manners at a time like this!' His voice was tight with anger.

'Patrick——' she slipped off the bed, touched the smooth skin of his back, but he pulled away from her. The muscles of his back and shoulders, she could tell, were tense.

'You're right. Not here. Not in Nikos's room with Nikos's girl!'

'I'm not his girl!'

He rounded on her, a shadow looming over her in the darkness. 'Oh, yes, you are. You're well suited, I told you that. I was a fool to ever think that you and I—we're bad for each other, Sara. Go to bed!'

When she stayed where she was, numb with misery, his voice lashed at her again. 'Look, sweetheart, I'm not made of stone—and I'm not an animal, whatever Sophia might have said. I'm a man—or hadn't you even realised that? Get upstairs and get to bed before I forget for the second time that Nikos is my brother, and do something we'll hate each other for in the morning!'

The coldness, the bitterness in the voice that had, only moments before, been murmuring her name, angered her. Tension crackled between them like electricity.

'Do you think it's easy for me to just—just—walk away?' she threw at him.

'Why not? You seem to be able to switch passion on and off to order. Little Miss Don't Touch me with the ability to become a panther when she wants to. Then——' his voice broke and he turned away from her again. 'I should have made an appointment—right time, right place. Go away, Sara. Just—go away!'

She went, stumbling blindly through the dark hall, up the stairs, into her room, tears running down her face. There she wept until there was nothing left except drained exhaustion.

When she woke the room was filled with sunlight. She lay still for a moment, then jumped up as she remembered the previous night.

Patrick had gone. All that remained of his presence in the villa was a damp towel lying by the front door, her dressing-gown a blue pool at the bottom of the stairs. Nicky's bed had been made neatly. Sara changed it, trying hard not to think of those brief moments when she had lain there, Patrick by her side. She put the towel and dressing-gown away, showered, dressed, made breakfast.

Then she went to the beach, and swam naked, giving herself gratefully to the sea's impersonal embrace. She swam until she was exhausted then went back to the house.

She felt lethargic, but the flame that Patrick had lit within her was still there. Her body ached for him—time and time again she wished she had gone back downstairs in the night, back to him.

Her common sense told her that she had done the right thing. Patrick was a man who only wanted passing affairs, whereas she could never accept that sort of relationship. But her common sense could do little to calm her skin, her lips, her hands, all clamouring to be with Patrick again.

'Did it upset you, being alone all night?' Nicky asked after lunch. They had come back full of high spirits, and he had glanced anxiously at her as she sat throughout the meal, hardly eating, hardly talking.

She tilted her chin, painted a bright smile on her lips. 'Not at all. I slept like a log all night,' she lied cheerfully.

'You don't look well, darling.'

The word jolted her out of her lethargy. Darling. That was what he had said on the phone. That was what had startled her so much in the dark, when she was in Patrick's arms, suddenly aware that she lay on Nicky's bed——

She gave herself a mental shake. 'I think I got too much sun yesterday. And too much wine!'

'Did Patrick give you a good day?'

The monastery and caves seemed a million years away. 'Lovely. I even learned some Greek dances.' The smoky taverna, Patrick's eyes as they danced——

'Terrific, aren't they? Patrick was always a good dancer. Let's forget about work for today, love——' he reached out, took her hand, studying her fingers. 'Sara, there's something——'

'I'd rather get on with the work,' she said, moving away, slipping her hand from his grasp.

'We can't afford to take too much time off.'

'Patrick didn't upset you yesterday, did he?'

'No.' She uncovered her typewriter, slipped a sheet of paper into it, opened a notebook.

'You're not——?'

'What?'

The word rattled from her lips. Nicky flushed, shook his head. 'Nothing. Forget it.'

But he watched her closely for the rest of the afternoon, and she was relieved when at last night came and she could escape to her room.

Patrick didn't come to the villa on the following day, or the day after that. Sara told herself bitterly that she didn't blame him—not after the exhibition she had made of herself that night.

His absence gave her a chance to assess the situation coolly as her fingers flew over the typewriter keys. Nicky's well-written dialogue covered sheet after sheet of paper before her eyes, and she didn't read a word of it.

She had to admit to herself that Patrick Laird had aroused her in a way that no man, even Richard, had done before. Now, Richard was only a vague memory, someone who had never really mattered.

She wanted Patrick. She made herself face the fact, humiliating as it was. But she could never have him, because all he wanted was a casual affair, and she couldn't accept that. She would have to put him out of her life and out of her mind now, for good.

Thoughts raced through her head as she went about each day, working with Nicky, swimming, sitting in the garden, talking, smiling, eating. And she realised that she must work hard on the script, must get it finished as quickly as possible, and get away from Corfu. Once she was home she would have broken all connection with Patrick Laird—and then, in time, the flame that he had lit within her restless body would die down.

'You got over Richard, and you can get over Patrick,' she told herself firmly as her fingers tapped out Nicky's script and page after page was added to the neat pile that was waiting to be checked and posted to London.

Only when she was alone in the darkness of the night did she allow the memories to creep back. Then she yearned to see him once more, to be held in his arms once more, before she flew back home.

Nobody else mentioned Patrick. Obviously they were used to him coming and going as he pleased.

Three days had passed without event before Nicky said lazily, 'Haven't seen Patrick for a while.'

He and Sara were playing backgammon in the garden after lunch, Sophia sunbathing nearby. She pushed her sunglasses to her forehead, blinked her large brown eyes at Nicky.

'Didn't I tell you? He's gone.'

The dice slipped from Sara's fingers and had to be retrieved from under a bush.

'What do you mean—gone?' Nicky squinted at the Greek girl, his eyes half-closed against the sun.

She propped herself up on one elbow, scanning Sara as she spoke, though her voice was casual.

'I met old Leonie in the village yesterday. Marina's ill, in Athens. She sent for Patrick, and—of course—he went to her at once.'

CHAPTER SEVEN

'Surely, Nikos, you must be finished all your work by this time!'

There was more than a hint of impatience in Hermione Laird's voice as she settled herself into a chair in her son's room. Nicky lifted his fair head from the book he was studying and eyed his mother with mild irritation.

'Not yet. Want to get rid of me?'

'I am anxious to spend some time with you. Is that unnatural? And I am sure that Sara is impatient to return home.'

Sara flushed. Hermione's resentment over Nicky's work had been growing over the past week. The last of the golden summer was upon them, and Hermione had more than once hinted that she wanted Nicky to join her in her mainland home, where she would pass the winter with a round of social engagements.

'There are a few scenes to be worked out—and the final polishing, of course,' Nicky pointed out. 'I want the script to be just right before it leaves me.'

'You work too hard, Nikos!'

'I work because I enjoy it—and I'm good at it. And that's why it has to be right before I'm finished.' There was a steely note in his voice now and his mother stood up, shrugging, her thick underlip jutting in a travesty of a pout.

'Very well. But remember that next month I close the villa for the winter.'

'Leave Sara and me here to finish the script.' There was mischief in Nicky's gaze now. 'We'll close the villa for you if you're in such a hurry to get away.'

Hermione glared at them both, then stamped out. Nicky laughed as the door closed behind her.

'Sometimes I think you're unkind to your mother. She really cares about you.'

'She fusses like a mother hen. She's got to learn that I'm independent. And that I've got my own plans. If only I hadn't been trapped in this place!' he slapped impatiently at his bad leg.

'You're almost ready to manage without your stick. It won't be long.'

'Yes. And then——' he stopped suddenly, then went on, 'Well, we'll see what happens then. Whatever it is, it isn't going to happen to please Hermione, that's for sure. Sara, let's take a day off tomorrow—just you and me. You can drive, I don't think I'm ready for that yet.'

She looked at him, dismayed. All she could think of was to get the script finished and leave the island.

'But you'll lose a day's work.'

'So what? Summer's almost over, and I haven't been out and about for weeks. One day—before the rains come. Just you and me!'

Once the idea was in his mind, she couldn't remove it. They set out on the following day, a picnic basket in the back seat, Hermione's unsmiling face watching as the car moved out of the short drive.

The weather was perfect, and Nicky relaxed noticeably as the miles grew between him and the villa. He directed her to a part of the coastline she hadn't seen before, to a small bay where the water creamed gently among small rocks and there was a sandy area where they could bathe.

Nicky was content to stay in the shallows, because his legs still hadn't the power needed for swimming. Sara stayed near him, and after a short while they came out of the sea, dressed, and went back to the car.

'You're a good driver,' Nicky commented as the car sped along a road that kept the sea in sight all the time. 'We should have done this before.'

Greek music rippled from the cassette player, reminding Sara of the taverna where she and Patrick had danced. Nicky was unlike his half-brother, talking and laughing freely as the car went on. Gradually, in his presence, the knots that had tied themselves in Sara's mind and heart began to loosen, and she recaptured the happiness she had first known in Corfu.

She parked the car on a grassy area off the road, and Nicky managed to settle himself on a stretch of warm soft grass.

'You'll have to pull me up again,' he pointed out. 'Or fetch help if I find I'm stuck down here?'

A few goats grazed in a nearby field, their bells tinkling gently. They were guarded by an old woman who sat with her back to a tumbledown hut, working on the ancient method of drop-spinning that the women of the island had been doing for centuries.

After they had eaten, Nicky half-dozed, his head on Sara's lap. He looked very young, and very happy.

'There's a timelessness about this place,' she said at last, her eyes on the black-clad figure of the old woman.

'Hmmm? Yes, I suppose there is. But I don't feel entirely at home here. My father was a city man and I suppose I am as well. I think it drives Hermione crazy to know that I don't care as much about Greece as Patrick does—and I'm the one who's half-Greek. If either of us settles here, it will be Patrick. Pity he and Hermione don't get on better together.'

'Why don't they?'

He shifted his shoulders into a more comfortable position. 'I don't know. Yes, I suppose I do. For a start, Hermione resented him. Patrick's parents were divorced and his mother went off with someone else and left him with our father. He was five at the time. And when Hermione came along—well, poor old Patrick got in the way. She didn't want to take on a stepson.'

'But that's unkind!' She spoke without thinking, her heart going out to the motherless little boy confronted by a cold stepmother.

'Patrick gave as good as he got. He and Hermione are alike, I sometimes think—stubborn, determined to have their own way. They both need to prove themselves. They both wanted my father's undivided attention—and then mine.'

'How do you feel about it?' she asked.

'I care about the two of them. Hermione's possessive, but she's my mother. She misses my father very much, though she'd never admit it, even to me. I wish she'd married again—but there was never anyone else for her. And Patrick—well, he's been a terrific older brother, always. There's a side to Patrick that you wouldn't believe existed.'

'Is there?'

'He's always helped me, believed in me. We'd do anything for each other,' Nicky said simply, and the land that Patrick wanted for Marina came into Sara's mind. She began to speak, then stopped. She had no way of knowing if Patrick intended to come back to Corfu, or if he would stay on the mainland with Marina. The thought of them together, somewhere far away, at that moment, hurt.

'He seems to care for Marina more than for anyone else,' she said abruptly, and Nicky's eyes opened, staring up at her.

'Why should you say that?'

'He's gone off to Athens because she's ill.'

There was a short pause. Nicky's eyes closed again, his face was impassive. Then he said, 'We all think the world of Marina. If I'd been fit, I would have gone to Athens to see if I could help. Let's go somewhere where we can see people, Sara—I can sunbathe at home!'

They drove to a small harbour town where they admired the luxury cruisers moored in the bay, and drank tall cold drinks sitting at a table in the busy little market place. Then they walked slowly along the main street, and Nicky insisted on buying Sara one of the beautiful gossamer-fine shawls the local women made.

He put it about her shoulders, a drift of cream foam against the blue of her dress. As he arranged it, the backs of his hands rested for a moment on her neck.

'Now you look like a painting,' he said, looking down at her, that intent look in his eyes again. She touched the shawl gently, thrilled by its beauty.

Later, they stood at a garden wall, watching a woman, her loom set up outside her door, working deftly on a similar shawl. Then they drove to Corfu Town, to stroll through narrow streets packed with shops.

When they got back to the car Nicky got in with a sigh of relief. Sara looked at him anxiously.

'Are you all right?'

He grinned at her. 'I'm fine. I just feel as though I've been on a marathon walk. But you have no idea how good it is to get out and about and feel like a person again, instead of an invalid!'

They headed back to the villa past olive trees with bundles of netting wedged in their branches, like arthritic old women carrying bales of cloth. Grapes hung from vines supported by trellises that roofed most of the small gardens, and lemons were like yellow lanterns on the trees.

Sara stopped the car and bought fruit from a roadside stall. They ate it a few miles farther on, parked high above a wooded valley.

'This is much better than working,' Nicky said with satisfaction, wiping orange juice from his fingers.

Sara, lying back in her seat, turned to smile lazily at him. 'Much better.'

'I wish we'd done this weeks ago. It's been great—a whole day together. But there's one more thing I wish I'd done a long time ago——' He reached out a hand and ran one finger from her hairline, down the side of her face, to her chin. Then he drew her towards him. 'I've wanted to kiss you for so long——' he whispered, and drew her into his arms. His lips were warm and firm on hers; they moved to her chin, her nose, her ears— light, tender kisses, before he gathered her close and kissed her properly.

There was none of Patrick's arrogance, none of the fierce gentleness that he had either. Nicky's embrace was warm, strong, and infinitely comforting, and Sara went into his arms willingly, returning his kisses, needing his strength near her.

When he finally took his lips from hers he kept her close, her head on his shoulder, his free hand stroking her hair. She felt the laugh in his chest. 'Now I wish more than ever that I'd taken the plunge weeks ago! But I was so afraid——'

She pulled back so that she could look up at him. 'Afraid of what?'

'Afraid that I might frighten you off. You seemed so—so reserved. And I didn't want to lose you through clumsiness.'

She sat upright, staring at him. 'Nicky, am I really like a prude? Is that what you thought?'

He pulled her back into his arms, kissed her, tucked her head into the hollow between his neck and shoulder again. 'I didn't say that you were a prude,' he teased, his voice happy. 'I said that you seemed to be reserved. An entirely different thing. Sara——'

'Hmmm?' She felt relaxed, contented, reluctant to move from his embrace.

'Stay on for a few weeks after the work's finished.'

The contented feeling slipped away. 'Nicky, I can't stay away from my office indefinitely. I might lose my job, and then what would I do?'

'You could always marry me—then you wouldn't need a job.'

She sat up again, and saw that Nicky himself looked startled at what he had said.

'Marry you? Nicky, you don't mean that!'

He grinned, shaking his head. 'Well, I didn't mean to say it just as soon—or just like that. But I've been wondering how to get round to the subject.'

'But I——'

'I think I'm in love with you, Sara,' he said quietly, seriously. 'I've been falling in love with you for a long time.'

She swallowed hard, seeking the right words. 'Nicky, couldn't we just wait until the script's finished, and then take things as they come?'

He started to laugh then, pulled her into his arms. 'Poor darling, everything's happening too fast for you! All right, I'll agree to a truce. But we'll get back to the holiday—and the proposal— when the right time comes!'

He was in high spirits for the rest of the journey, and when they arrived back at the villa Hermione looked at him sharply, then at Sara.

'Nikos, you have been overtired!'

'Rubbish,' her son grinned at her.

'But you look—different——'

'Just a dose of fresh air,' he brushed her anxiety aside. Sophia looked up from a magazine and studied them both.

'Perhaps they just had a good day,' she suggested, silky-voiced.

'A very good day,' Nicky assured her cheerfully.

Hermione said no more, but once or twice Sara
looked up to find the older woman's eyes resting
thoughtfully, coldly, on her. Each time Hermione
looked away quickly. Nicky seemed to be quite
unaware of his mother's scrutiny. He looked
better than he had since Sara had arrived at the
villa, even she could see that.

The hurt that Patrick had left with her, the
hunger for him, had eased during her day with
Nicky. She felt at peace again, though there was
the problem of Nicky's proposal. But it had been
an impulse on his part, and she felt sure that he
wasn't entirely serious about it.

'You must have had a very enjoyable picnic
yesterday,' Sophia suggested the next morning in
the kitchen.

'What makes you say that?'

Sophia was squeezing juice from an orange. She
had come downstairs in a black lace negligee that
hid little of her beautiful body, and her hair was a
careless mass of curls about her face. She had the
look of a predator.

'He looks so happy, even this morning. I
think you have made a conquest, Sara.' She
tipped the juice into a glass and leaned against
the wall, watching Sara over the rim of the glass
as she drank. Sara went on with what she was
doing.

'Am I supposed to cheer about it?'

'I think so. After all, Nikos is going to be a rich
landowner one day. What you might call a good

catch. If you are careful. I think that his mother would have liked him to marry a Greek girl, like me. But I do not find Nikos exciting enough. I need an exciting man,' said Sophia with a deepening of her voice, almost like a cat about to purr, Sara thought savagely.

'Like Patrick?'

She realised her error just as the predator pounced, a swirl of black and gold.

'So you find Patrick exciting?' Sophia moved forward. Sara felt her face grow warm, bent her head over the toast she was buttering.

'I don't know anything about the man. I'm going by what you told me yourself.'

'Oh—that!' Sophia, robbed of her prey, sounded disappointed.

'Do you mind opening the door?' Sara picked up the tray and smiled sweetly.

'No, I didn't mean Patrick.' Sophia opened the door and moved ahead of Sara, tossing over her shoulder, 'He's not really exciting enough for me.'

'Who isn't?' Nicky limped out of his room. 'Good morning, Sara, you look gorgeous today.' His eyes approved as they took in the yellow sleeveless dress she wore, caught at the waist with a gilt chain.

'Nobody you know, darling,' Sophia assured him carelessly, moving into the lounge as though she was on the catwalk at some big fashion house. Nicky stopped to let Sara go in before him, dropping a swift kiss on the back of her head when Sophia's back was turned.

Hermione and Sophia both decided that they needed some shopping from the village after lunch. As Hermione maintained that she was busy, and Sophia never actually went into shops and bought things for herself, it fell to Sara to go. As they both had sizeable lists, she had to take Nicky's car. She decided to go soon after lunch, when the day was at its hottest and not many people were about. That way, she could shop quickly and get back to the villa.

She stacked the groceries and fruit on the passenger seat, wrinkling her nose at the stuffiness in the car. A cold drink would keep her going until she reached the villa again.

Thinking longingly of the cool terrace at the back of the little taverna, where she could sit in the shade and watch the waves come in, Sara turned from the car—and stopped short.

A battered, familiar Land Rover was parked opposite the lane where Leonie lived. Even as Sara recognised it, Patrick Laird and a girl who could only be Marina emerged from the lane, heading for the truck.

Marina wore black jeans and a pale green sleeveless tunic top, cut low to show smooth brown skin. In the photographs Sara had seen, her hair had been long. Now it was cut short, night-black and thick. Patrick's muscular tanned arm was about the girl's shoulders, and as he lifted her into the Land Rover they laughed into each other's eyes. Then he shut the door and stood for a moment, talking to Marina.

Sara's heart thumped, lurched sickeningly, thumped again. She finally managed to start moving, backing to the door of her car, fumbling for her keys, praying that she would escape unnoticed. Just then, possibly attracted by the swing of her buttercup-yellow skirt against shadow, Patrick turned and saw her.

He spoke to Marina, waved at Sara, and began to walk towards her. Panicking, she managed to open the car door and jumped in. She heard him call her name as she pushed the ignition key into place with trembling fingers. The engine started, roaring its protest as her foot pressed the accelerator. In the rear view mirror she got a glimpse of Patrick running towards her, waving. He wore crisp new jeans, a navy shirt open at the neck to show a thin gold chain. His hair was tousled and his face puzzled as the car began to move. He stopped, fists on hips, looking after her as the car drove too fast along the narrow street and round a corner. Tomatoes rolled from their bag and landed splashily on the floor as she straightened the wheel.

She took a different road, turning away from the villa, watching in the mirror until she was sure that he wasn't following her. Then she drew in to the side of the road and stopped the car.

Her hands were trembling as she gathered up

the spilled fruit. Of course he wouldn't waste time following her—the land Rover had been facing the other way, and obviously he and Marina had some outing planned, possibly to see the land earmarked for the children's home. Why on earth would he have followed her anyway?

'Idiot!' she told herself time and time again, waiting until she had calmed before going back to the villa. Why did she have to scurry away in fright like a sheep running from the wolf? Why couldn't she have stopped and talked, met Marina, behaved like a responsible adult? Patrick already had a poor opinion of her—today's exhibition would not make it any better.

If the others knew that he was back, they said nothing. Sara found herself waiting for the noise of an engine slowing and dying outside the gates, but nothing happened. She watched for a tall, broad-shouldered figure walking down the driveway, anticipated the moment when a buccaneer would fill the doorway and come back into the lives of the villa residents. But nobody called, and the calm of the house went on undistrubed.

In bed that night she rehearsed the things she would say when he arrived. She would be cool and collected, adult, sensible. She fell asleep to dream that he and Marina had arrived, and that everyone was laughing at her as she stammered and stuttered in his presence.

By the afternoon of the following day she was so tense that she was incapable of working properly. The waste-paper basket was filled with crumpled sheets of paper, torn angrily from the typewriter. She had been working all day at a task that would normally have taken her an hour.

'What on earth's wrong with you, darling?' Nicky asked in lazy amusement as she pulled another spoiled page out of the machine and tore it up.

'It's this typewriter—no, it's not, it's me. I'm just having an off day, I expect.' She rubbed aching eyes.

'Go and have a swim.'

But she shook her head. 'Not today.'

'Come into the garden, then———'

She jumped up, gathered papers noisily, went to the filing cabinet. 'I'm all right—just let me get on with what I'm doing, Nicky!'

'Come here———' he held out his arms, drew her to him, stroking her hair. 'Calm down, darling, you've been edgy all day. What's bothering you?'

She took a deep breath, closed her eyes. 'Nicky, I want to go home.'

'Home? You mean—to London?' There was dismay in his voice. She nodded against his shoulder, and he lifted her chin so that she had to look at him. 'But why? I thought you were happy here. Is it my fault? Did I overdo things the other day—say too much?'

'Of course not. It has nothing to do with you, Nicky.'

He frowned. 'But something's happened, I can

see it in your face. Is it Sophie? I know she's a
vindictive little so-and-so at times, but I thought
you could handle that. Or has my mother been
talking to you? If so, I want to know, Sara!' His
voice hardened, his eyes grew angry.

She pulled away from him and turned to the
window. It looked out on to the side garden where
flowering shrubs were a mass of helio, red and
yellow in the sunlight. 'Nobody has said anything,
honestly. It's just——'

It was just that she couldn't bear to go on playing a cat-and-mouse game with Patrick any more.
Now that Marina was on the island with him, she
had lost all chance of being alone with him again.
And even if she was, she would probably spoil it
for them both. The thought of seeing him again,
with the others there, terrified her. She had to get
away, as soon as possible.

'Just what?' Nicky's bewildered voice said
from behind her.

'I'm—I'm homesick.' It was a feeble excuse.

His hands touched her shoulders. 'Oh, darling!
Homesick for a shared flat and an English
autumn? Listen, we'll have a wonderful time here
once the script's been packed off. You and me,
Sara—like the other day. Remember?' His fingers
tightened their hold.

'I know—I'm sorry, Nicky, but all at once, I've
been here long enough——'

He turned her to face him. 'Sara, please—just
stay until the work's finished, then we'll go back

together. Don't leave me—not now!'

'You don't understand——' she said despairingly.

'No, I don't. All right, if that's the way you feel, we'll go back now, together. As soon as we can arrange two seats on a flight out. Okay?'

'But the script! And what would your mother say?'

'I can't finish the script here without you, darling. We'll take it back with us, finish it in London. And Hermione can say what she wants, I'm not going to let you go on your own. Whatever it is that's bothering you, I want to be with you. I'm going to stay with you no matter what it takes, until you send me away. BecauseI love you.'

Then she was in his arms, clinging to him, seeking comfort from his strength, his closeness.

'Nicky——'

'Ssshh!' He held her, his lips on her hair. 'Sara, being with you is all that matters. Nothing else is important. It's all right, darling, I'm holding you—everything will be all right now, my darling——'

And it would be all right. She knew that, feeling his hard, warm chest against her cheek, his arms holding her tightly. Nicky would never frighten her, never anger her—he cared, he would always care. But at the same time she knew that she couldn't let him offer her so much without knowing the truth.

As she lifted her face to his his gaze rose beyond

her head and his arms slackened slightly. Sara turned, still in his embrace.

Patrick seemed to fill the whole doorway, his hands tense on the frame at each side. He wore a scarlet sweater under an open brown jacket, and his hair was neater than usual. His lips were curved into an amiable smile but his eyes, as they moved from Nicky to Sara, holding her gaze, were a brilliant, cold cutting blue.

'I'm sorry——' he said, and his voice, too, had an edge of cold steel beneath its drawl. 'I didn't realise I was bursting in on something important.'

CHAPTER EIGHT

SARA tried to move away from Nicky as Patrick came into the room, but Nicky held her against him.

As Patrick cleared the doorway, Hermione appeared, mouth tight as she saw her son and Sara together. Patrick moved towards them, hesitated, turned and pulled Sara's desk chair into the middle of the room. He straddled it, arms folded on the back, and by the time he looked up again, his expression had changed to one of mild interest.

'You weren't interrupting,' Nicky said casually. 'You might as well both know now—I've asked Sara to marry me.'

Hermione's gasp drew Sara's attention to her, away from Patrick. She was aware that she herself had gasped. The Greek woman sat down as though her knees had given way, a hint of grey showing that she had paled beneath her brown skin.

'Nikos!'

'I knew you'd be pleased, Hermione,' said Nicky, the hard note back in his voice. 'You like me to be happy, don't you?'

Sara felt as though she was living in a night-

133

mare. Her own voice, as she pulled away from
Nicky's restraining hand, was over-loud in her
ears. 'I haven't given Nicky my answer!'

'But of course,' said Patrick gently, 'you'll
accept him.'

Then Nicky's arm was about her shoulders
again. 'I hope so. And we're going back to
London as soon as we can arrange it. Sara wants
to see her family again—and make arrangements.'

It was all being taken out of her hands. Patrick's
eyes, when she dared to look at them again, were
polite, friendly, interested. The brothers seemed
to have everything under control, while Sara and
Hermione were brushed aside. Patrick rose, put
his hands on Sara's shoulders, kissed her cheek
briefly, formally.

'Welcome to the family, little sister,' his deep
voice said, and he released her and stepped back.
'Well, this calls for some sort of celebration.
Champagne, anyone?'

'There's some in the fridge—just in case.'
Nicky made for the door, but Sara followed,
anxious not to be left alone with the other two.
'I'll get it, Nicky——'

'I will bring it.' They had forgotten about
Hermione. Now she rose with a dignity Sara
had never seen before, went out, reappeared a
few minutes later, when they had moved into
the lounge, with a tray of glasses and the
bottle.

Nicky opened it and they drank the toast. The cold liquid flowed down Sara's throat, but she hardly noticed it. A second glass helped to bring her to her senses. It seemed to be all right. Hermione had proposed a toast 'To my son and to his future wife'. She had managed to say it, had managed to smile. Sara admired her for her self-control.

And Nicky and Patrick seemed perfectly relaxed. Sara began to come out of the state of shock. Perhaps it was for the best—perhaps this was the answer to the strong attraction she felt for Patrick. Nicky had at least made it possible for her to get over the first moments in Patrick's presence.

'We'll have to have a proper celebration,' Patrick was saying now, cheerfully. 'Be my guest tomorrow night, we'll all go out to dinner.'

Plans were made, times discussed, while Sara and Hermione sat dumbly by.

'If you drive out there together,' said Patrick, 'We'll meet you. Save a lot of coming and going.'

'We?' Nicky raised his eyebrows.

'Marina and I.'

There was a very short, very intense pause. It lifted Sara out of the faint daze she still felt.

Hermione broke it. 'I did not know that Marina was on the island,' she said sharply.

'You didn't?' A curious expression flitted over Patrick's face as he looked from Hermione to

Nicky. Then he turned to Sara, his eyes faintly puzzled. 'I—I thought you might have heard, on the grapevine.'

'No.' Nicky sat on the sofa beside Sara. 'When did she arrive? How is she?'

'We came together, two days ago. And she's better now. She wasn't at all well—overwork. You'll see her tomorrow evening. She was asking about you.'

Sara wondered, if Marina had been such a close friend of Nicky's and Sophia's, why she hadn't been to the villa earlier, why she wasn't there that afternoon with Patrick. Hermione was looking at Nicky now, her eyes hard as black pebbles.

'Well, I'd better get back. She's waiting for me,' Patrick said easily, putting his empty glass down. Sophia arrived just as he was leaving. She stepped, gazelle-like, from a sports car which roared off again, the blond young man at the wheel waving farewell as he went. There was amusement in Sophia's eyes when she heard the news of the engagement, but she passed no comment.

During dinner she and Nicky kept the conversation flowing, and afterwards Hermione pleaded a headache and retired to her room. Sophia kept the other two company in the lounge, playing music, playing backgammon, talking. It was late before she finally went to bed and left Sara and Nicky alone.

'Why did you do it?' Sara asked as soon as the door closed behind Sophia's elegant back. Nicky took her in his arms and kissed her before he said, 'Do what, darling?'

'Tell everyone about us!'

He pulled her down to sit beside him on the sofa. 'It seemed like a good idea at the time. Seriously, I just wanted everyone to know. Is that so wrong?'

'But—but I haven't said yes yet!'

He stared at her, then roared with laughter, pulling her into his arms. 'My darling, neither you have! Well, say it now.'

'Nicky——'

'You're not going to turn me down, are you?' There was anxiety in his voice. 'Darling, you can't. Not now, not after——' He stopped, took a deep breath. 'I'll be glad to get away from this place.'

'Why should you want to leave?'

'Why should you?' When she made no reply, he went on. 'All right, we both have our reasons. But I want to go. Arrange a flight tomorrow, will you? And once we get back to London, we'll be free to finish work, talk about ourselves, get things sorted out. All right?'

'All right.'

His arms closed about her with a new intensity. 'Oh, Sara,' Nicky whispered, against her throat, 'I do need you—more than you realise!'

She slept well, but woke early the next morning. For once the room wasn't splashed with sunlight. When she went out on to her small balcony, it was to see that the sky was overcast, the sea sullen and oily in the grey light. The weather suited her mood.

She dressed in a white sweater and dark blue trousers, brushed her hair, put on a little lipstick, and went downstairs. Nobody else was up, so she let herself out quietly and wandered round the garden. The path down to the beach was gloomy, but she went down the steps and walked between the trees, glad to put the house behind her for a few moments.

The rocks, normally warm and friendly under the hot sun, seemed to frown at her. She felt like an intruder on the silent, sulking beach. She walked to the edge of the water, then stifled a scream as a voice behind her enquired, 'Can't I go anywhere without being reminded of you?'

She spun round, Patrick sat on a flat rock, his back against a rocky wall that towered above him. Elbows on knees, he was contemplating a stone that he held in one hand. As Sara stared at him, he took aim and flipped the stone out to sea. It bounced once, twice, and again and again before disappearing under the surface with a dull plop. In the distance the Greek mainland was hidden by a wall of grey, she noticed, as she watched the path taken by the stone.

'What are you doing here?' She thought of leaving, then decided that she would only look like a sheep again. He selected another stone, studied it, ignoring her until he had satisfied himself that he had the right stone.

'I'm thinking. I always come here when I want to think.'

She sat near him. He skimmed the stone across the water and selected another. The sea and sky seemed to meet and merge, both grey. The wall advanced across the water towards them, and she realised that rain was on its way.

'Ever been out to that island?' Patrick nodded to a lone clump of stone at the mouth of the small bay, almost eclipsed in mist.

'No.'

'We spent a lot of time there as kids. It's grassy in the middle—good for sunbathing. Well, congratulations again. You hooked my brother.'

He wore off-white trousers, white sneakers, a gray sweater. It fitted in with the weather. Even his eyes, as he finally looked at her, seemed to be gray, very like Nicky's, and with the same intent look. Only his tanned face and black rumpled curls gave him colour.

'I did not hook your brother.' She tried to keep her voice level. There was no point in quarrelling with him, not now.

'I see. You just happened to fall into his arms, and you just happened to be thinking of something . else when he announced your engagement, so you forgot to tell him he was wrong.'

'I haven't told Nicky I'll marry him! It was—it was all——'

'A mistake?' He gave a short laugh. 'Come on, love, you know as well as I do that the evidence was more than circumstantial.'

'What are you complaining about?' she shot at him, stung by the sneer in his voice. 'You're the one who insisted that we'd make a good couple, aren't you?'

He tossed the next stone into the water a few feet away, his mouth in a tight line. The muscle jumped at his jawline. 'And you're the one who insisted that I was wrong. The other night, you might have told me that things were getting serious between you and Nicky. Instead, you coolly led me on, and then—no wonder you got into a panic when you thought I was going to seduce you in his room!'

'But I—'

'Oh, don't keep protesting your innocence, it gets boring after a while!' he threw at her, getting to his feet. 'I said it already—congratulations. As you kept telling me, I'm not a very good judge of women. I thought that you just might be someone special. Well, I was wrong, wasn't I?'

He stormed across the shingle, refusing to stop when she called his name. She caught up with him, caught his arm, pulled him round to face her.

'Patrick—you've got to listen to me! That night

in Nicky's room, I was a fool. I behaved badly. I wanted to tell you, but you'd gone to Athens, to Marina. And when you came back——'

His face was unforgiving. Behind him, she could see rain pocking the smooth gray surface of the sea, moving inch by inch towards them.

'When I came back, sweetheart,' he said, his voice icy, 'you ran like a startled deer from me. You ran back to Nicky!'

'I ran because——' She was holding the front of his sweater, shaking him, trying to make him understand. 'Patrick, I'm so confused! I have to make you understand how I feel about you——'

'I know how you feel about me,' he said. 'You made it very clear. You haven't an ounce of feeling for anyone, Sara. You fooled about with me, lost your nerve when I took you seriously, and you caught my brother on the rebound——'

'You—you——' She would have attacked him, but he was holding her wrists, laughing without amusement, towering over her.

'That's more like the real Sara. Well, I expect you and Nikos will be good for each other, darling. I didn't kiss you properly yesterday, did I? Well, the others were watching. But here's wishing you a happy future——'

His arms were cruelly hard as they closed around her, crushing her to his chest. And his lips held hers brutally in a bruising kiss that held no warmth. He was like a stranger, and she was suddenly afraid, suddenly aware that they were quite alone, that nobody would see or hear them. She fought, panic-stricken, against him.

When he finally released her she fell back a step, fingers to her mouth, eyes horrified as she stared up at him.

'More than you can cope with, love?' he asked coldly. She turned from him and ran towards the trees and the path back to safety, back to Nicky. Slipping and stumbling on the stones, she ran, hardly aware that the rain had reached the beach, and was falling in a sheet of water.

She had reached the first trees when Patrick caught up with her, spinning her round and slamming her against a tree-trunk so hard that she cried out.

'I hadn't finished with you!'

'Patrick, please——'

'It doesn't take long to break your brittle shell, does it?' He pinned her against the tree with his body, catching her chin in one hand as she tried to turn her head away, forcing her face round to meet his lips.

Rain hissed in the trees as Patrick's mouth fastened on hers once again, seeking, demanding, taking with a vindictive satisfaction. His hands wrenched at the white sweater, explored her body with all the merciless greed of the pirate he often reminded her of. She tried to make her mind a blank, tried to be passive under his attack, tried not to let herself be aware of his touch. But the tiny flame that had responded to him before flared up in her, pushing reason and sense out of reach. Her treacherous arms lifted, her hands touched him, held him. Her mouth responded to his as her body strained against him.

She felt the anger leaving him, felt a tiny tremor run through his arms. He lifted his head and looked down into her face, bewildered. Then with a low murmur he gathered her to him and claimed her lips. The fierceness, the anger, had gone, replaced by a mutual passion that locked them together. Patrick's body throbbed against hers, and she answered his need with her hands, her arms, her lips. Rain sluiced down on them from the trees, plastering their hair to their faces, soaking their clothes, and they didn't notice.

Roughly, Patrick pulled the neck of her sweater aside so that he could bury his lips in the warm hollow of her neck. The anguish of the past week left Sara, to be replaced by pure joy. Her searching hands slid under his wet sweater to caress the smooth, muscular back. And in answer, he lifted his face to hers again to kiss her with passionate tenderness.

When at last he drew away from her, he looked dazed. She felt so weak that she was glad of his strength, still holding her against the tree. And she could tell that he, too, was shaking.

'My brother seems to have found himself a

pretty wonderful lady,' Patrick said finally, his voice husky and strangely unsure of itself. Rain dripped from the tree on to her upturned face; she closed her eyes against it, and felt his lips touch her closed lids very gently.

'Patrick—about Nikos——' she started to say, and right on cue Nicky's voice called from above. They both turned, looked in the direction of the villa, then back into each other's eyes. Patrick drew a deep breath and stepped back, releasing Sara. 'It's Nikos. You'd better go to him,' he said bleakly.

'But——'

'Sarah?' The voice was clearer now. Nicky must be at the top of the steps. Patrick pushed wet hair out of his eyes with both hands and looked down at Sara again as though he was coming out of a dream.

'Go on—if he tries to come down the path when it's wet he'll fall. And I don't want him to know I'm here.' And he walked quickly out of the shelter of the trees and across the beach without looking back.

Nicky had reached the foot of the steps when Sara met him. His face cleared when he saw her. 'There you are, darling—I began to worry when the rain came on and you didn't come back.'

'I was walking down by the sea. I—I tried to shelter under a rock.'

'You look as though you've been in the water with your clothes on!' He pulled her into his arms and kissed her. 'You taste good—all rainwater and flowers. Come on, you'd better get into dry clothes.'

The rain had gone off by the time she stepped out of the bath. She towelled herself vigorously, every inch of her glowing body remembering Patrick's embraces. Slowly, she put on a pale blue dress, with long sleeves and a demure collar. Her hair, still damp, was left to dry itself, and when she examined her face in the mirror she was surprised to find that her lips weren't swollen and bruised from his kisses. True, there was a glow in her eyes, but the others could, and would, put it down to the fact that Nicky and she were supposed to be engaged.

Nicky was eager to get on with as much work as possible, and Sara was happy to fall in with his plan. But as she worked Patrick was never far from her mind. She had to admit to herself now that her feelings towards him were more than the physical attraction she had first imagined them to be. She loved Patrick Laird, loved him and wanted him with an unbearable intensity. And he—he would be off to Brazil soon, and then he would turn his thoughts to Marina and the convalescent home.

She sighed, slipping another sheet of paper into the typewriter. Her only course was to go home with Nicky, to give herself time to think things out and then, probably, to tell Nicky that she could not marry him.

At that moment Nicky passed her chair, bending clumsily to kiss her cheek, and she had to resist the impulse to go into his arms, to tell him everything and hope that he would comfort her. With Nicky lay security, comfort, gentleness; the sort of future she once dreamed of. If she couldn't tame his dark, tempestuous brother, why shouldn't she marry Nicky?

She thought of life as Nicky's wife—thought of meeting Patrick as a member of the family, entertaining him, perhaps staying at times under the same roof as him, while married to his brother. And knew that if she could not belong to Patrick, her only course was to cut herself off from everyone and everything connected with him.

With that thought in mind it was difficult to prepare for the celebration dinner. She had brought one good dress with her for evening occasions, but had never worn it because of the quiet life they lived at the villa. Now she put it on, a soft dress of deep rose with a low, rounded neck, loose bodice, gathered waistline, and tiered, full skirt. With it she wore the creamy soft shawl that Nicky had bought her.

Sophia wore a plain dress, white, low-cut to show her beautiful breasts and slim waist to best advantage. Her honey-coloured hair was caught back with a wide white bow, giving her a deceptive innocent air, belied by the sultry brown eyes and the full red mouth.

Hermione pleaded a headache, and announced that she would have to stay at home. Nobody seemed unduly surprised, though Nicky, elegant in a light-coloured suit with a brown high-necked sweater under it, looked tight-lipped for a moment. Then he shrugged and put one arm about Sara, one about Sophia.

'We'll celebrate without you, then,' he said lightly, and his mother, without another word, stamped upstairs to her room.

They went in Hermione's car, with Sophia at the wheel. Night had fallen by the time they got to the restaurant decided on by Patrick and Nicky.

Patrick came to meet them, but it wasn't until they were in the restaurant, under the lights, that Sara got the opportunity to look at him. He laughed when he saw the surprise in her eyes.

'Well, you did ask me once what I looked like when I dressed up. I thought that this was the perfect chance to show you.'

He wore a dark suit, crisp evening shirt, bow tie. His hair was well brushed, and he looked devastatingly handsome.

Sara's heart flipped over as she looked at him. He barely glanced at her, taking her in from head to toe in one searing look before turning to his half-brother.

'Come on, Marina's waiting to meet you.'

Nicky's hand tightened slightly on Sara's elbow as they followed Patrick and Sophia to a corner table. Then they had reached Marina, and there was a flurry of greetings.

Marina was as lovely in the flesh as she had been in the photograph standing in her grand-mother's house. Her eyes held a hint of sadness, but the warmth that brimmed her small, perfect face was unmistakably genuine. Her hair curled in a neat cap, her neck was long and slender, her movements graceful. She made Sophia look as though she was made of plastic, Sara thought unfairly.

Sara found herself swept into an embrace.

'I have been looking forward to meet you,' Marina told her in prettily-accented English. 'Welcome to Corfu, and many congratulations.' She turned to kiss Nicky, reaching on tiptoe. 'Nikos is a very wonderful man, and I know that he will make you happy.'

She wore a loose full-length dress in shades of orange and yellow. In the artificial light she looked like an exotic flower blooming among more hardy blooms, and more than one man turned to glance at their table, attracted by Marina's beauty and vitality.

Sara hardly tasted the meal or the wine. Patrick seemed to be completely at his ease, and it was hard, as she looked across at him, to imagine that only a few hours before they had been locked in a passionate embrace in the rain. He was attentive towards Marina, making sure that she had enough to eat, that she had wine, which she hardly drank—caring for her with a tenderness that made Sara's heart ache.

When they danced, Patrick and Marina moved together gracefully, absorbed in each other, gazing into each other's eyes.

'Only a few more weeks, and then I'll be able to dance again,' Nicky said longingly as they watched the others. A friend dining at a nearby table had claimed Sophia as a partner, and she moved sinuously in and out of the throng with her panther-like grace.

'Do you like dancing?'

He nodded, laughed. 'Isn't it strange, darling—we're going to be married, and we still don't know much about each other. Yes, I love dancing. I hate to sit here and watch others when I can't get up myself. When I'm back to normal, next summer, we'll come back to Corfu and I'll teach you the local dances. We'll have a wonderful time!'

She doubted that she would ever return to Corfu now. The island's magic had soured for her. The ancient Greek gods that haunted the place, turning it into a paradise on earth, had ranged themselves against her, showing her a deep pleasure that she had never imagined possible, then taking it from her with cruel delight. She never wanted to see Corfu again.

'Sara, may I have this dance?' Patrick loomed over her.

'I'd rather stay with Nicky.'

'Go on, darling——' Nicky urged her. She would have protested, but Patrick's grip on her hand forced her to rise and follow him on to the small dance floor without further ado. He took her into his arms, holding her formally.

'So you managed to recover from this morning's—interlude,' he said, smiling politely down at her. When she didn't answer, he went on, 'I'm sorry, that was crude of me. And I'm sorry about this morning, too.'

'Sorry?'

His eyebrows rose. 'Of course. I presume you've been bristling all day, waiting for an apology. Well, here it is. I had no right to do what I did, to say the things I said. I'm sure that you and Nicky are ideal for each other, and I behaved like a spoiled child.'

'It did take two of us,' she pointed out tartly, and he hesitated, then laughed, steering her past a plump couple who almost blundered into them. 'Yes, it does—but I had no right to take advantage of you, or to frighten you. I was in a black mood. My fault—and I don't think we should talk about it any more.'

Sophia danced past them with yet another partner. Sara caught a glimpse of Nicky and Marina at their table, talking earnestly to each other. Then the music ended, and Patrick escorted her back to her seat. The matter was finished, he had made that clear, and as far as he was concerned, there was nothing more to be said.

The evening dragged on. Sara drank more wine than she would normally have taken, and managed to dull the misery within her heart. She and Patrick danced again, but this time in silence.

Finally Patrick ended the celebration party.

'You're tired, Marina,' he said with concern. 'I knew that this would be too much for you.'

She smiled up at him, accepting his ministrations as her right. 'I am all right. You fuss over me more than my grandmother does, Patrick. But I think that Nikos should go home now—you look pale, Nikos.'

She lifted one small hand and touched his cheek, but Nicky pulled away, almost irritably. 'I'm fine. Though I think it's time to call it a day.'

Patrick tucked Marina tenderly into his sports car and roared off into the night with a casual wave to the others. Sophia drove Hermione's car expertly over the dark roads, while Sara sat in the back, in the circle of Nicky's arm. His protecting, comforting arm, that could no longer shut out the memories, the pain, the wanting.

The villa was in darkness. Sophia went straight to her room, kicking her shoes off as she went. Someone would collect them in the morning for her. Nicky kissed Sara, a long, hard kiss, outside her bedroom door.

'I love you, Sara,' he whispered fiercely into her hair. 'I'm going to make you happy!'

In her own room she dropped her clothes on

the floor, changed into a nightgown, and went out on to the balcony. The heaviness of the early morning had gone. The air was clear, cool, almost silent. She couldn't even hear the waves below. A sudden breeze rustled the trees that had overhung her earlier, when she had been in Patrick's arms. All at once, she felt very lonely.

CHAPTER NINE

'I THINK that it is time for us to talk,' Hermione Laird's heavy voice cut across the rattle of the typewriter.

It was the day after the celebration dinner. Nicky had gone to the nearest town with Sophia, taking the wheel for the first time since the accident.

'It isn't far, it's a good road, and Sophie's with me,' he had brushed his mother's protests aside. 'I've got to start driving some time, and the sooner the better. Don't fuss, Hermione!'

But she had fussed right up to the minute when the car disappeared round a corner and vanished from her sight.

Now, hovering over Sara like a black-clad angel of doom, she went on, 'Perhaps you will come into the lounge and drink some wine with me.'

Protests were waved aside with an impatient movement of one squat jewelled hand. In the lounge Hermione brought glasses of the sweet wine which she loved, and sat opposite Sara, looking at her intently.

'We should know each other better, should we not? I know nothing of your family,' she said imperiously, a modern-day Queen Victoria.

'My parents are ordinary people—I live in a flat, and there's really nothing else to tell,' Sara tried hard to keep an even note in her voice.

'Do you not have to consult with them? After all, marriage is a very great step for someone so young and—unversed in life.' Her voice was insulting, contemptuous. 'Will your parents be happy that you will spend most of your life in Greece, far away from them?'

Sara took a sip of wine, realised that her hands were shaking with suppressed rage, and lowered the glass quickly. She knew that the older woman had seen how the glass trembled, knew that Hermione thought that she was nervous.

'I'm old enough to make my own decisions. And Nicky spends most of his time in England.'

Hermione's lips tightened. 'I intend to change that. I have land—business—in Greece. Nikos must now help me to look after it. After all, it will go to him one day. He will become a wealthy man—but of course, you already know that, I am sure.'

Anger flooded through Sara, and she knew that if she was not careful she would say something that might hurt Nicky. She put the glass down and got to her feet. 'Mrs Laird, I am not marrying your son because he has money. I pity you if you think that his only attraction is his wealth. You obviously don't know Nicky. If you'll excuse me, I have work to do——'

'I think that we have other things to discuss,' Hermione's hard, flat voice stopped her as she was about to open the door. 'I must be honest with you and tell you that this engagement must be broken—at once.'

Sara turned. 'Because you say so? Mrs Laird, has your son no right to make his own decisions?'

Hermione rose to her full height. 'My son is easily led astray. There have been—others. I have protected him from them all. I love my son, and I know——'

'You do not love your son, Mrs Laird.' Sara ignored the woman's gasp of rage, ignored the warning voice in her own brain. 'You would free him if you loved him. I think he feels caged and hemmed in when he's with you. I don't even know if he really cares for me. It may be that he wants to marry me because it's one way of breaking out of this prison that you've created for him with your so-called love. You're not losing him to me—you're losing him because you insist on holding on to him, treating him like a possession, refusing to accept him as a person. He's real, Mrs Laird. He's a warm, caring wonderful human being, not another few acres of land or a diamond ring!'

There was a short, horrified pause, then, 'You dare to speak to me like this?' Hermione spat the words at her.

'You're right. I'm being unpardonably rude to you in your own home. But it's time someone spoke up for Nicky, time someone told you what you're doing to him!'

'You are impertinent!'

'You forced me to speak my mind.'

Hermione's voice was a whiplash, searing Sara's mind. 'You do not love Nikos! I know you—anyone would do for you. Why Nikos? Why not someone of your own kind? Why not Patrick?'

'I'm not what Patrick wants. I'm ordinary—too ordinary for him. And if you really want to know the truth, Patrick's worth a dozen of you, Mrs Laird. If you had ever given yourself the chance to get to know him, you'd be aware of that. But you were so wrapped up in Nicky, so busy trying to get him all to yourself, that you had no time for Patrick, had you? What do you want to do with Nicky? Keep him away from women for ever? Arrange a marriage that he'll hate? Because I warn you, if you try to mother him for much longer he'll break loose. And if he doesn't marry me, he might choose someone even more unsuitable than I am.'

'You——' said Hermione, gray-faced, 'will never marry my son.' She began to advance, beside herself with rage. Sara backed away, came up against the wall. The woman's eyes were murderous, her voice vicious. 'I will see to it that you will never——'

The door opened.

'Mind if I come in?' Patrick asked lightly, cheerfully, beaming from one to the other. 'I'm looking for Nikos.'

Hermione stopped, took a deep breath, turned to pick up her empty glass and put it on the table with neat, precise movements. 'Nikos is not here.'

'Ah.' Patrick smiled slightly at Sara, eyes narrowed. 'Bad timing, as usual. Well, I suppose I'd better get back to the village. I'll call in later——'

As he turned to the door Sara made a slight movement towards him, longing to call him back. Strangely enough, it was Hermione who said, 'Patrick, don't go.'

He turned, eyebrows raised.

Hermione forced a smile. 'Poor Sara has been working so hard this afternoon. I thought that you could perhaps take her for a drive.'

He blinked at her. 'Oh, I doubt if Sara would want to go for a drive with me, Hermione——'

'I'd—I'd like to go out for a little while,' Sara interrupted, and he shrugged.

'If you want to. Won't be long, Hermione.'

The sun was a golden blanket, and it seemed to Sara as she walked out of the villa that the room she had just left was black and cold, filled with evil. She welcomed the warmth, the light outside.

Patrick's small blue car was an oasis of normality. He drove away from the village, saying

nothing. A breeze whipped Sara's hair about her
flushed face, cooling it, easing the tension that
knotted her. Patrick glanced at her once or twice
but kept quiet until half an hour later, when he
stopped the car outside a small village taverna.

'Ready for a drink?'

It was cool and quiet inside. The proprietor
served them, then returned to the table where a
group of men conversed noisily. A couple of children played at another table, their dark eyes intent
on the toy cars they raced over the plastic surface.

'We're going to be left in peace,' said Patrick
with satisfaction. 'So—what's troubling you this
time?'

'This time?'

'Don't snap at me, Sara, and don't deny that
every time you and I meet one of us is uptight
about something. Not that I have to look far for
the cause this time. Hermione can be mean when
she puts her mind to it.'

'Mean? She was—she was——'

'All right, I know what she was.' His teeth
gleamed white in the shade of the room as he
grinned. His hand closed comfortingly over hers
on the table. 'Spit it out—I'm already the black
sheep, so you can't say anything that I haven't
already heard.'

'Your stepmother,' said Sara furiously, 'has the
mind of a supermarket cash-till!'

He laughed. 'Not bad!'

'She's decided that I'm marrying her precious

son for his money.' Sara glared at him. 'And you can't fault her for that, because you think the same thing, don't you?'

He released her fingers to spread his large, capable hands on the table, palms up. 'Now wait a minute, sweetheart—don't class me with Hermione. I merely thought you were being very sensible in marrying Nikos. He's secure— and he wants you as his wife. Hermione's the one who's making it all sound nasty and underhand.'

'The sooner we're away from this island, the better!'

'When do you go?'

'In five days' time. That's why she's trying to scare me off, I expect. Time's running out.'

'Are you going to tell Nikos—about the things she said to you?'

She shook her head, and Patrick relaxed.

'I wouldn't want to hurt him. Not in any way.'

'That's my girl. By the way, I was boorish last night—again. I didn't tell you how lovely you looked. And you did. Nikos is a lucky man.'

'Patrick, about Nicky——'

He cut across her quickly. 'He loves you, Sara. He'll be a wonderful husband—just what you need.'

'Will he?'

He took her fingers, playing with them, his head bent. 'Yes, he will. He needs someone like you, Sara. I know I haven't helped matters, fooling about the way I did, but I'll keep out of the way now, I promise.'

'Patrick——' She almost told him, but as though he knew what she was going to say, he interrupted again.

'Oh, I won't deny that I find you very attractive, Sara. That temper of yours—I've never met anything quite like it. But on the other hand, what would it have meant? A week in Paris, something like that, and then—finish. And you wouldn't go for that sort of relationship, would you?'

It hurt to say it, but the thought of being with Patrick for only a short while was as hard to bear as the thought that she had already lost him. 'No, I wouldn't.'

The muscle jumped. 'So.there you are,' said Patrick, releasing her hand and smiling into her eyes. 'You stick with Nikos. You'll be happy— and I'm not around very often, so you won't be irritated by me.'

'And the land?'

His eyes widened. I'd forgotten about the land! Any chance of you having a word with Nikos before you go?'

'Why not?' she said as lightly as she could. 'Now that I'm almost one of the family, it should be easier. Tomorrow—I'll talk to him tomorrow. I might even take him to see it, if you tell me how to get there.'

'I've got a map in the car.' He signalled to the proprietor, who brought two more drinks. 'I'd really appreciate it if you could help me, Sara. It would be good for Maria to be here, to be doing something that made her happy. If I can't get that children's home under way, I'm afraid she'll just go back to Athens and work herself to a stand-still.'

'But surely you don't need the land to persuade her to stay?'

He frowned across the table at her. 'Persuade her? What are you talking about?'

The proprietor put two tall, chilled glasses in front of them, and Patrick paid him. Sara waited until the man had returned to his cronies.

'Marina—surely you don't need to bribe her to stay with you?'

Patrick, about to take a drink, put the glass down and stared at her. 'Sara, you confuse me at times. You're always pushing Marina's name in front of me. What in the world are you getting at?'

'You—in love with Marina.'

'I love a lot of people,' said Patrick. 'I'm a loving and lovable man, or hadn't you noticed? No, I don't suppose you have. But let that pass. What makes you think——' he stopped short. 'Sara, have you been listening to Sophia again?'

'I don't know what you mean by "again". I only——'

'Sara? My dear Sara, what has the girl told you this time?'

There was a pause. 'That you've always been

in love with Marina. That Stavros proposed to her before you did, and now——'

He laughed so hard that the children jumped and the men in the corner looked up from their talk. Sara stared at him, totally confused. Finally he sobered, and said gently, 'But, Sara, you don't mean to tell me that you hadn't realised? You didn't know?'

'Realised what? What should I know?'

'It wasn't me who wanted to marry Marina, Sara. It was Nikos.'

Then he asked, concern in his voice, 'Are you all right, Sara? I didn't mean to——'

She forced a smile to her lips. 'I'm fine. I just—of course, that's why Marina never comes to the villa!'

'That's why. Hermione put a stop to it before poor Nikos got as far as a proposal. Then Stavros and Marina were married, and that was that.'

'If only I'd known——'

'Love, it's over. Nikos is going to marry you, there's nothing between him and Marina now.'

But she wasn't so sure. Now she understood why Nicky had suddenly wanted to leave Corfu. The two of them—Nicky fleeing from Marina, she herself fleeing from Patrick, turning to each other for comfort. Now it was her turn to laugh.

'What's so funny?' asked Patrick.

'Hermione——' she lied. 'Like a guard dog, warning women away from Nicky one after the other. But why are you so keen on the children's home, if you aren't in love with Marina?'

'Because I'm very, very fond of her—I always was. She's that sort of person. But she wouldn't consider me as a husband. Marina has impeccable taste. I want to help her because she and Stavros were two wonderful people. The home was their dream. Is it so wrong to just want to make Marina happy?'

'No.'

'You know, you really must learn not to take everything Sophie tells you with a pinch of salt,' Patrick added.

'Why should she lie to me? What pleasure does it give her?'

He shrugged. 'She's bored here. She likes to cause trouble, it amuses her. It always did. But I can't think why she went to the bother of setting you against me. She must know that there's nothing between us.'

The conversation was getting into deep waters. 'What happened between Nicky and Marina?' asked Sara.

'I think he was on the verge of proposing to her, and then Hermione found out about it. She did everything she could to come between them, including throwing Stavros and Marina together. The inevitable happened—Stavros proposed, Marina accepted, and poor old Nikos was left out in the cold. She would never have managed to bulldoze me like that. But then, she wouldn't bother—I'm not her son.' A bleak note had crept into his voice, and Sara saw that his face was blank, his eyes shuttered.

'Perhaps Marina would have turned Nicky down,' she suggested.

He blinked, and the remote look vanished. It was as though he had come from a dream. 'Perhaps. I don't think so, though. Marina was very fond of Nikos, and when she realised that Hermione was putting pressure on him she made a point of staying away, to save him embarrassment. I think Nikos took it as a bit of cold-shouldering. I did what I could to patch things up, but Hermione was determined. Oh well, it's all water under the bridge now. But you managed to take Hermione by surprise.'

He chuckled, and she asked suddenly, 'Is that why you insisted to me that Nicky and I would make an ideal couple? So that you could annoy Hermione?'

His eyes flashed blue fire at her. 'Is that what you think? Good God, girl, surely you——' he stopped, bit his lip. 'Of course not. If I want to annoy Hermione I just turn up on her doorstep. That does it.'

'But surely Nicky would get that land for Marina, since he felt so strongly about her.'

'Like a shot,' his half-brother agreed. 'But Hermione would oppose it even more. In a way, his being engaged to you might help. And I think you're able to cope with Hermione—from what I heard today.'

Colour stained her face. 'You heard us?'

'It was difficult not to.'

'How much did you hear?' she demanded, remembering her defence of Patrick.

He gave her an enigmatic smile. 'Enough to know that Hermione's going to have her work cut out as far as you're concerned. Come on, I'd better take you back now.'

In the car, he fished a map out from under the dashboard and showed her the road leading to the land they had visited together. He took her hand, using her finger as a pointer to mark the road, and at his touch a wave of longing swept through Sara. She pulled her hand back as soon as she could, and Patrick glanced at her in swift surprise before saying formally, 'Well, time to get back, then.'

His lips were set in a firm line as they drove to the villa, and she knew that he felt rejected. No point in trying to explain anything, she thought drearily as the lovely countryside sped by the window. She would probably not see him again, and it was too late for explanations.

Nicky was waiting outside the gate, sitting on a tree-stump. He got up as the car stopped.

'I thought you were only going to be out for half an hour, Sara.' His voice was accusing, his face expressionless.

'My fault——' Patrick said casually, and made to lean across Sara to open her door. But Nicky already had it open, and had taken her hand in his.

'Coming in for a cup of coffee, Patrick?' she asked automatically.

'We were planning on having dinner early,' Nicky cut in. 'Some friends of Hermione's are coming over.'

Patrick looked thoughtfully from his brother to Sara, then back at Nicky.

'In that case, I'll be on my way. Thanks for your company, Sara. Sorry I took her away for so long, Nikos.'

Nicky said nothing, but as they stood there he put an arm protectively, possessively about Sara. She could feel his unaccustomed tension, standing close to him. Patrick eyed them both narrowly for a further moment, then the car started off and turned on to the road. Sara watched it until it was out of sight. Patrick did not wave, or look back.

'Just what was all that about?' she asked as they went into the garden.

'I could ask you the same question.'

She stopped, stepped out of his embrace. 'Nicky, I don't know what you're talking about.'

'I think you do.' His voice was low, taut with suppressed anger. 'I came home, expecting to find you here—and instead I discover that you're out joy-riding with Patrick!'

'But——' she got no further. The door opened and Hermione stood there, magnificent in black lace and gold ornaments.

'Sara, my dear!' Her voice was warm, her smile brilliant, her eyes triumphant. 'We have been so concerned—we thought that Patrick had taken you away from us for ever!'

Looking up at her, as she stood regally at the top of the steps, Sara suddenly realised that Sophia wasn't the only person in the villa who could weave a tissue of damaging lies from an innocent act.

There was no time to talk to Nicky. The visitors were expected almost immediately, and Sara only had time to have a quick shower, change into a simple tunic dress of pale lilac silk, catch her hair back in a knot, and put on some make-up before the villa was ringing with the voices and laughter of the arrivals.

During the meal, Nicky and Sara were silent, while Hermione and Sophia sparkled. Now and then, lifting her head, Sara caught a malicious gleam in her hostess's eyes. She felt awkward, ill at ease in the presence of a group of people she didn't know. They spoke Greek and Nicky, caught up in his own thoughts, rarely bothered to interpret for her. As soon as possible she escaped to her room, and nobody seemed disappointed to see her go.

She had just reached the safety of her room and started to unzip the back of her dress when there was a tap at the door.

'Sara? I want to talk to you.'

She stared at the closed door, anger bubbling up in her. 'Tomorrow.'

'Tonight!' The door opened and Nicky came

in. Sara pulled the dress back on to one shoulder.

'I have to talk to you,' he said shortly, closing the door. 'Sara, why did you go with Patrick this afternoon?'

She thought of Hermione's triumphant smile, and decided to walk carefully. 'Why not?After all, I spent an entire day with him the other week—and that was your idea.'

'You weren't my fiancée then!'

'Nicky, when you got back today, what did your mother tell you about me?'

'That Patrick had called, and you had gone with him. Well? Was she right?'

So that was why Hermione had insisted on her going out with Patrick. Sara chose her words carefully. 'Not exactly. Patrick called to see you, not me. I didn't mean to be away for long—we just drove, stopped for a drink, and then came back.'

'Was that all?'

'Of course that was all.'

He came to her, put his hands on her shoulders, staring down at her. His eyes were unhappy. 'Patrick's a good-looking man. He's—charming—all things I never could be——'

'What did your mother tell you about Patrick and me, Nicky?'

His fingers bit into her shoulders. The dress, unfastened at the back, slid off one shoulder again. 'Sara, is there anything between you and Patrick?'

It wasn't a lie, so she could say it, looking up into his tormented face. 'No, there isn't.'

He pulled her to him, kissed her lips, her throat. The dress fell to her waist, and he drank in the sight of her tanned, rounded breasts cupped in a wisp of white lace. 'Sara——' He loosened the knot of hair, and buried his face in it as it swung in a scented cloud round her face. An answering thrill ran through Sara as his lips sought hers again. Then, as his fingers edged the strap of her bra from one shoulder, she remembered Patrick's hands, his lips, his passion. And she knew that she couldn't give herself willingly to anyone else while the memory of him was so strong.

'Nicky—no!' She pushed him away, pulled the dress around her again. 'Not—not here, Nicky.'

For a moment she thought he was going to insist, then he nodded. looking around the room. 'I know. Not in this house. God, Sara. I wish we were back in England, away from this blasted island——'

When he had returned to the others downstairs, Sara changed into nightgown and robe and went out on to the balcony. She knew why Nicky wanted to get away from Corfu. She knew, too, that whatever Hermione and Patrick might think, Nicky still wanted Marina.

She sat for a long time, looking out over the trees. The sky was clear, pricked with stars that gleamed bright and cold.

Two lonely people—herself and Nicky. Two

people who could not get what they wanted, and had turned to each other for comfort. It might work.

But she knew, as she at last went to bed, that until she got Patrick out of her mind and out of her heart, it would never work.

CHAPTER TEN

'I don't know why we had to come all the way out here,' Nicky protested with lazy amusement.

They were sitting on the grass overlooking the spot Patrick had earmarked for the children's home. In the two days since Sara had last seen Patrick, Nicky's work on his script had finished. All it needed was some re-typing—and in another two days they would be aboard the plane, on their way back to England. It had been easy enough to persuade Nicky to come out for a drive, because his mother's presence in the villa was like a shadow hanging over them all.

'I wanted you to see it.'

He lay on the grass, half-asleep, looking very young and vulnerable. 'I've seen it hundreds of times before. We own it—at least, Hermione does.'

'I know. Patrick told me.'

At the sound of his brother's name, Nicky opened his eyes. He had gone out of his way to be as loving as possible to Sara since their quarrel over Patrick, and she had taken good care not to mention the name in his hearing.

'What has he got to do with it?' Nicky asked now, suspiciously. He put out a hand, tried to pull Sara down to lie on the grass with him. 'Darling, don't spoil it all. Here we are—there's the sun and the blue sky, not a soul to be seen. Just you and me, alone at last——'

'Nicky, listen to me. I want to tell you something,' she interrupted firmly, and he groaned and closed his eyes.

'Go ahead—get it over with, then we can get on with what I've got in mind.'

But as she spoke, describing the home, Marina's dream, the plans she had made, Nicky's eyes opened again, and he began to follow her with deep interest. When she finished, he was propped up on one elbow, looking over the land.

'Who told you all this? Marina?'

'Patrick.'

'So that's what the two of you had to talk about,' Nicky said softly. 'And all the time I thought—but why didn't he tell me? He knew I'd get Hermione to sell the land. She doesn't need it!'

Sara didn't answer, and after a while he nodded. 'I see. He didn't want me to fall foul of Hermione, or get tangled up in a row between them. If only Marina had told me earlier!'

'I don't think she wanted to cause trouble for you either. And as far as I can gather, you haven't seen a lot of her for—for some time.'

Nicky picked a blade of grass and snapped it in two. 'You're right. It seems that a lot of trouble has been taken to avoid friction between me and

Hermione. So what does that make me, Sara? Do they all really think Hermione has such a hold on me?' His voice was angry.

'They did what they thought best——'

'I know, I know. But you can't deny that I'm being sheltered, protected, by them both. Well, that's not going to be necessary now,' said Nicky with new vigour. 'Help me up, love, I'm still a bit stiff. I want to have a walk around here, and find out just what Patrick has in mind.'

Together they walked round the land while Sara explained as best she could, Nicky grew more enthusiastic.

'If it's what Marina wants—and if Patrick's going along with it, then it must be a good idea. Are there any plans? I'd like to have a look.'

'In Leonie's house.'

'Let's go, darling. If we're flying out in two days' time there's no time to lose!'

When they reached the car, Nicky asked, 'Let me drive. I enjoyed being behind the wheel again the other day. I'll take it slowly, I promise.'

Sara handed over the keys and got into the passenger seat. As the car moved on to the road and Nicky settled at the wheel, her heart lightened. Marina was going to get her land, and it looked as though Nicky was going to make a stand against his mother. At least something was working out.

Remembering his determination to get the home for Marina, Sara wondered if perhaps, before she left Corfu, she could nudge Nicky's thoughts in Marina's direction. The door that Hermione had slammed between the two of them was open a crack. It might be possible to give them another chance.

She looked down into a valley and saw a battered Land Rover nosing along the road below, on its way to meet them. Her heart flipped over. She didn't want to meet Patrick again! But on the other hand, it was almost time for her to go home, and everything that had to be said between her and Patrick had been said. There was nothing to fear, other than the heartache which was going to be her companion for some time to come.

She stole a sidelong look at Nicky. 'I think Marina would be happier living on Corfu.'

He nodded. 'She belongs here. Patrick was right.'

'It's funny,' Sara said idly, intent only on putting Marina into his mind as much as possible, 'but when I first heard of Marina, I got it into my head that Patrick wanted to marry her. It was so——'

'What?' Nicky turned to look at her, startled. The wheel turned in his hands, the car swerved, straightened, swerved again, out of control.

Sara screamed as the wheels on her side went off the road with a jarring thud. The car hit soft ground inches below the roadway, and the steering wheel bucked crazily as they slid sideways, with terrifying speed, towards the sheer drop to the valley below.

The world turned upside down, something hit
Sara's knee sharply, something else exploded in
her head, and then the noise stopped as though
someone had turned an 'off' switch, and there was
only the sound of screaming.

'Slap her face!' a woman said, far away, and a
deep voice nearer at hand protested, 'I can't do
that!'

'Slap her!' the woman repeated impatiently. A
stinging blow jolted Sara out of the crazy night-
mare of noise and confusion. The screaming
stopped, and she was grateful for that. Then she
realised that it had been coming from her.

Worried blue eyes were close to hers, someone
was holding her. 'Sara? Darling, are you all
right?'

To her horror, she burst into tears. Arms held
her, rocking her as though she was a child.
Patrick's voice murmured comforting, nonsensical
words in her ear. It was wonderful, and she never
wanted it to stop. Then all at once she remembered the car, the accident, and pushed the
enfolding arms away, struggling to sit up.

'Nicky—what happened to Nicky? Is he——?'

'Ssh!' he tried to soothe her. 'He's all right—at
least, I think he is. What about you? Can you
move?'

His hands moved over her, gently, without
passion. With his help she stood up, shakily, and
discovered that she was all right, apart from a
bruised knee.

'I hit it on something—the dash, I think——'
She looked round, holding on to Patrick.

'Come and sit down.' He lifted her, carried her
easily, set her down on the grassy verge of the
road. 'Are you sure you're all right? We came
round that corner there, saw the car going—my
God, Sara——' he caught her to him, his face in
her hair, 'I thought you were going over the
edge!'

She looked beyond him to the grassy slope. The
car was lying at an angle against a tree, the driver's
door open. Nicky was there, slumped back in his
seat. Marina, in a cream-coloured shirt and pale
blue jeans, was leaning in the door.

'Nicky!'

Patrick straightened up. 'I—we think he's all
right. Just stunned. Stay there, I'll go and help
Marina.'

He ran across the short stretch of grass to the
car and after a moment Sara felt strong enough to
follow him. She was shaking all over, and still felt
dazed, but she was all right.

Patrick was easing Nicky out of the car.

'I thought I told you to stay where you were!'
he snapped at her. Nicky's eyes were closed, his
face white under its tan. Blood caked one side of
his face, and smeared Marina's shirt. As Patrick
began to lift his half-brother clear, Nicky stirred.
Patrick laid him gently on the grass and they all
bent over him. Marina's small brown hands
checking him efficiently.

'No bones broken, but I think he has concussion——'

Nicky opened his eyes, looked at Sara, then at
Marina. The glazed look cleared as he saw the
Greek girl.

'Marina?' he whispered, then, his voice growing
stronger, 'Marina! But——' he tried to turn his
head 'where's Stavros?'

Patrick's hands clenched painfully on Sara's
shoulders. She stood up, and Nicky didn't notice
the movement. Marina took his hand, talking
quietly to him in Greek.

Patrick took his jacket off, put it about Sara's
shoulders as she shivered. Then he looked up as a
lorry came round the corner, followed by a car.
They both stopped, and men came swarming out,
talking, pointing, running to them.

'Hang on, love,' said Patrick with a grin, 'I
think the cavalry has just arrived.'

Hours later, Patrick handed a glass to Sara as
she sat in the lounge at the villa.

'Here, try this, you need something. You look
terrible,' he said with brutal honesty. She felt terrible. The reaction from the accident had set in,
and the glass shook in her hand.

A car door slammed shut, and he glanced out
of the window.

'Oh-oh, here comes Hermione. Stay where you
are, Sara.' He went into the hall, and she heard a
torrent of Greek, Hermione's voice shrill, frightened, Patrick's decisive. Then the door was

thrown open and Hermione was bustled in by a
firm hand under her elbow.

'—far better if you leave him to sleep,' Patrick
was saying. Hermione's face had lost its colour,
and her eyes blazed as she saw Sara.

'It was you!' she hissed. 'You did this to my
Nikos!'

'That's enough, Hermione!' Patrick's voice
cracked, his eyes blasted the small plump woman
with merciless blue fire. 'Sara had nothing to do
with it. She's lucky she escaped with her life!'

Hermione rounded on him, screaming in her
own language, and he caught her wrists, holding
her without much effort.

'In English, Hermione! And if you take my
advice——'

The door opened again, and Marina appeared
at his back. 'He's sleeping now. He'll be all
right——' she stopped as she saw Hermione.

'Sit down!' Patrick pushed his stepmother into
a chair. 'And stay there!'

Surprisingly, she stayed, staring at Marina.
Patrick poured out two liberal doses of brandy,
gave one to Hermione and one to Marina.

'Listen to me, Hermione. Nikos was driving the
car, it went off the road, he managed to stop it
before anything serious happened, and he's suf-
fering from mild concussion. He is sleeping now,
and I'd advise you to leave him alone until the
morning, when the doctor will call. All right?'

There was another torrent of Greek, directed

in turn at them all. Marina bit her lower lip, and Patrick answered his stepmother in her own tongue. He spoke at length, and Sara had no way of knowing what he said, but it had considerable effect. Hermione deflated like a balloon, sinking into her chair, head bent.

'Now, I'm going to take Marina home. And you, Sara, are going to bed.' He stood up, put one arm about Marina, held out his free hand to Sara. In the hall he looked down at her, a slight frown between his dark brows.

'Can I trust you to go to bed right now and sleep? Or do I have to put you to bed myself.'

'I'm going.' She dragged the tattered remains of her self-respect round her. 'Patrick, what did you say to——'

He laughed shortly. 'Don't ask. I said things that should perhaps have been said a long time ago. Poor Hermione, I hurt her. But it had to happen. She won't give you any more trouble. Go to bed, Sara.'

She nodded, turned on the stairs as they were going out. 'Marina? You'll come back tomorrow— to see Nicky?'

Marina, tired and childlike as she leaned against Patrick's broad shoulder, looked up at him, then smiled at Sara, a wide, warm smile.

'If you think I should——'

'I think you should,' said Sara, and left them standing in the doorway.

Marina came on the following day, but Patrick

was not with her. Sara, stiff and sore after the jolting she had received in the accident, moved her typewriter to her room, and began to work on the last part of the script.

She hoped against hope that Patrick would appear, but there was no sign of him. Marina stayed for a large part of the day, closeted in Nicky's room. Hermione went about with a closed face and tight lips.

On the following day Sara stacked the typescript into a neat bundle late in the afternoon, closed the typewriter, and went downstairs.

Hermione came from her son's room just as she reached the hall.

'Nikos would like to talk to you,' she said formally. He was still in bed, a large lump of sticking plaster on his forehead.

'Sara? Why haven't you been in before?'

She took his hand, bent to kiss him. 'I've been busy. I finished the typing. It's all ready to take to London when I go tomorrow.'

'Tomorrow! I forgot about——'

'I cancelled your seat on the plane, Nicky.' She sat by the bed. 'I'm flying out alone.'

'A fine ending to your trip to Corfu,' he tried to smile, and failed. 'Sara, I don't know where to begin. That accident—as the car was going over, I remembered the other accident. I remembered——'

'I know, Nicky. You don't have to tell me.'

He played with the sheet. 'It was my fault—Stavros, everything——'

'Did you blame Patrick when everyone thought it was his fault?'

'No, of course, not! But——'

'Nothing has changed, Nicky. You just know more about it, that's all.'

The smile was easier this time. 'Bless you, Sara, you always put things the right way. I really needed to know you. Well, I'm going to stay on here for a while. I'm taking over the responsibility for the children's home. Patrick's leaving in a couple of days—Marina needs someone to help her with the administration, and the finance.'

'What about your mother?'

The smile broadened. 'Oh, she's going to have to get used to changes. It might even do her good.'

'Nicky—remember when you asked me to marry you?' she said carefully. 'Well, I didn't get the chance to reply. I'm sorry, Nicky, you're a wonderful person, but—I have to turn you down.'

Nicky pulled her down and kissed her. 'You're a wonderful person too,' he said when he had released her.

Another beautiful evening arrived, her last island evening—and Patrick didn't appear.

'He has been very busy working on the convalescent home,' said Marina when Nicky mentioned Patrick's name. 'He will come when he is free.'

Sara's suitcase and travelling bag were waiting in the hall early the next morning. The light dress and jacket she planned to wear on the trip lay across her bed. She got up early for one last swim, one final memory to take home with her.

The beach looked as though nobody had ever set foot on it. Remote, wild, beautiful, it settled under the blue sky, accepted the first caresses of the day's sun, already warm.

Sara dropped her robe and stepped down into the water. It was like glass—and, as it received her into its embrace, like silk. It twined itself round her body, held her gently on its surface, soothed her. She wanted to stay there, to forget about the plane and home and everything else.

The island waited for her at the mouth of the small bay. Patrick had talked about it. This was her last chance to see it. She swam out, long, slow strokes, in no hurry to reach the rock that thrust itself from the middle of his looking-glass magic sea.

She reached it, put a hand up to catch hold of a handy spur of rock, then gasped and almost slipped beneath the surface as a strong hand caught hers. A dark head appeared over the shelf of light-brown rock above her.

'We do meet in the most unusual places,' said Patrick. 'Coming aboard?'

He lifted her easily on to the island where she sprawled, gasping, on the warm shelf of grass that made up the centre of the small rock.

'You might have drowned me!'

'I'd have dived in and saved you.' He stretched full-length and grinned up at her. He wore deep blue trunks, and his body was tanned, lithe, relaxed.

'What are you doing here?'

'The same as you, I imagine. Having a swim before the rush starts.' He indicated the silent empty beach across the water. It was just visible to someone sitting up—the rock encircled the grassy area, hiding it from view.

She squeezed water from her hair, pushing the wet strands back from her face. Already the sun's warmth was on her naked shoulders and arms.

'Seriously, though, I wanted to say goodbye to you. I've been busy, and I know you're leaving today. Without Nikos.'

'He's still in love with Marina. That was plain to see when he came round after the accident.'

'And you're leaving them together. Poor Sara! Are you very upset about it?'

She shook her head. 'Not a bit. I told you that Nicky and I weren't meant to marry.'

'I'm not often wrong,' he mused, shaking his head. 'So you're fancy free again, are you?'

She looked down at him, turned away from the lazy amusement in his eyes. 'I suppose so.'

To her horror, she felt a hand sliding gently, tantalisingly, along her back as she moved to study the beach.

'Pity you and I weren't on the same wavelength,

Sara,' said Patrick. 'We could have had a lot of
fun.'

She closed her eyes, willing him to take his
hand away. But he didn't, and his touch sent a
thrill racing through her entire body.

'I'm still interested, if you are——' he let the
words hang in the air. One finger found her spine,
crept up it.

She thought of the plane, of home, of the flat,
the agency. It was all so gray. Then she couldn't
think of anything but his touch, his presence
inches away from her. She couldn't bear to turn
and look at him in case he saw the longing on her
face.

'I might be——' she said through stiff lips.
There was a slight pause, then—'You mean, you'd
be willing to——' there was surprise in his voice.
She felt him lifting himself up on one elbow,
heard his voice in her ear. His fingers reached the
strap of her bra.

'Yes.'

'You and me—a week in—anywhere at all?'

She nodded. Tears stung the back of her eyes.
But it was too late to dive into the water, to swim
to the safety of the beach, to take that plane and
fly out of his life. Even a week—she would settle
for an hour, if that was all she could get.

His hand slid under the strap. 'It would be
quite a week,' he said thoughtfully. 'But you know
what I'm like, don't you, Sara?' His lips brushed her
shoulder. 'Not like Nikos. After that week——'

'I know,' said Sara, and was surprised at how steady her voice was.

The fingers flipped suddenly, and the bra loosened, fell to the grass. Patrick's hand was warm on her back, his fingers closing gently over her shoulder. She closed her eyes, willing him to take her into his arms, and at the same time silently begging him to go away, to leave her alone, free of the sweet torture that he was capable of inflicting on her with his mere presence.

'And what would you do then?' Patrick breathed in her ear. She took a deep breath, swallowed hard. She had to play the game his way now. She had committed herself.

'Oh——' she said lightly, denying the tears that wanted to fill her eyes, 'after that—there'll be other men, other weeks——'

There was another pause. His hand stilled, then his thumb gently caressed the nape of her neck.

'Oh, I couldn't go along with that,' he said at last. 'I'm not a very patient man, Sara, I'd insist on a divorce if you behaved like that.'

'Divorce?' She turned so quickly that she almost overbalanced and he had to catch her in his arms.

'Divorce,' said Patrick sadly.

'You—you mean——'

'I mean,' his voice was muffled now in her hair, 'I mean that you've won. All those years, determined never to let myself be caught by one

186

woman—and then you came along.'

He held her away from him, his eyes lingering on her face, drinking in every feature lovingly. She had never seen such tenderness in his look, even when he spoke about Marina. 'I tried to stay away after the accident. But I couldn't bear to think of you flying out of my life.'

The smile curved his mouth again. 'Darling, don't stare at me like that. You've won—I give in. Sara, I love you.'

She still couldn't believe it. 'For ever?'

'For ever and always. I love you, and that's the first time I've said those words to anyone. My darling, I'll never stop saying them to you—and only to you.'

'But——'

'Stop fussing, and kiss me!' he commanded, and she went into his arms. He laid her gently down on the grass, and when at last his mouth released hers they were both breathless. With a laugh, Patrick picked up the wispy red bikini top and tossed it towards the sky. It hung there for a moment, then fluttered out of sight, into the sea. Patrick looked down at Sara for a long moment, his eyes devouring her.

'Oh, my love——' he said at last, a groan in his voice, and she opened her arms and gathered him close.

Then she remembered—'Patrick, I've got to catch a plane——'

His body pinned her to the ground. His skin,

warmed by the sun, slipped softly, deliciously against hers.

'There's time to catch the plane. We'll get to the airport, don't worry.'

'We?'

He drew back slightly. 'Of course. You don't think I'm going to let you out of my sight now, do you? I booked a seat last night, when I realised that I couldn't live without you. We'll go back to England, get married, you can make arrangements, and next week we leave for Brazil. Darling, how do you like the idea of a honeymoon on a construction site in Brazil?'

Sara tangled her fingers in his thick black hair. 'It sounds wonderful!'

'I promise you,' said Patrick tenderly, 'It will be. Oh, my darling, don't ever move out of my arms!'

His hands explored her with the possessive touch of a welcome lover, and she answered his lips, his fingers without hesitation.

A voice soared across the water.

'What was that?'

'Ssh!' he murmured into her shoulder. 'Pay no attention!'

But the voice called again, and Sara, impatient at this intrusion into their happiness, sat up and looked over the sheltering wall of rock. Patrick wound his arms about her, resting his chin on her shoulder.

'It's Mrs Laird. Patrick, she must be trying to

let me know that it's time to go to the airport!'
Sara stared, fascinated, at the dumpy little figure
dancing about on the shingle at the water's edge.

'Oh, let her know that you understand, and
she'll go away.' He waved at his stepmother, then
tried to push Sara back on to the grass.

'Darling, she's waiting. We'll have to go—we
must get that plane!'

'If you insist. Race you to the beach——'
Reluctantly, he rose, stepped on to the rock ready
to dive.

'Patrick!'

'Now what?'

'I can't go to meet your stepmother like this!'

He stood there, a Greek god, running his eyes
over her naked breasts. 'I don't know—I think
you look beautiful. I thought that the first time I
saw you. You should give up wearing clothes at
all.'

'Patrick!'

He sighed, looked reluctantly at Hermione's
distant figure, then at the wisp of red cloth drift-
ing placidly out to sea on the surface of the calm
blue-green water. Then he stooped and kissed
Sara, a warm, possessive kiss.

'Just this once. But don't go away until I come
back. You're mine now, and I'm going to make
sure I keep you.'

A faint breeze gusted across the water, riffled
his black curls, hurried the bra further away.

'If only Hermione could have minded her business just once,' he said regretfully, longing in his blue gaze as it travelled slowly over Sara.

'Patrick—please?'

'Oh, hell!' said Patrick, and dived, in one beautiful movement, into the glassy waters.